# Under a Comanche Moon

# and Other Stories

Rickey Pittman
Bard of the South

Published by BookLocker.com, Inc., Bradenton, Florida.

Printed in the United States of America.

BookLocker.com, Inc.
2014

First Edition

The hard questions are simple . . . but the answers are hard, and
hard to remember

—Auden

# Table of Contents

# Preface

These seventeen stories came about as a result of my interest in and exploration of history, and themes related to human nature, love and loss. Some of the stories confronted me with the darker side of my own and others' natures. Some stories are colored or shaped by localities I have lived or traveled through. Others are the result of my observations of people and the serendipity of discoveries in my research. When I look at the list of these stories, I'm looking at twenty years of my life.

My literary career began with a life-changing reading in my freshman composition class in college of Ernest Hemingway's "A Clean Well Lighted Place." That short story pushed me into the world of literature. There have been other writers since Hemingway who have shaped me by their short stories—many others.

I've read many of these stories in public venues. It is my hope that the reader will find these stories interesting, perhaps even helpful in his or her own quest to understand human nature or develop one's own writing.

There are so many who have been of invaluable help to my writing—many of whom spent many hours reading, editing, discussing my manuscripts and characters, and encouraging me on those days when I was discouraged or struggling to try to make my writing work. Without friends like these, I never would have found my voice and developed my craft. I especially thank Billy Dunn, an excellent writer, who did more than anyone to help me develop the craft of writing.

# Under a Comanche Moon

## May 1864

"I am a cemetery by the moon unblessed."
— Charles Baudelaire

Micah and Elbert stopped in front of the first Fort Worth saloon they came to. When the war started, they had enlisted in the 23$^{rd}$ Texas Cavalry, and this was their first furlough, the first opportunity in two years to return to their families in Parker County. Micah looked up at the full moon. During his years with the Texas 23$^{rd}$ he had watched the moon wax and wane, much like the Confederate armies he had fought with. It hung there in the sky like a harbinger of death. He had listened to the Louisiana soldiers talk of the moon's beauty, heard one quote a poem about it, but Micah hated the moon. The full moon was a reminder, a terror. In his mind, he saw his house in Jack County bathed in blue light, Erin inside sewing or reading or cleaning. He saw his twins, Skye and Benjamin, playing together near the fireplace. Outside, this same Comanche moon would be illuminating the garden, the neglected fields, and the surrounding buttes. He tried not to imagine dark savage eyes in the darkness spying on his family.

Micah said, "I know a tracker by the name of Chicolithe. He works at Camp Ford tracking down escaped prisoners. He said he saw a Comanche outside of Tyler once."

"I wondered how long you could go without talking about Comanches or Kiowas," Elbert said. "You're eaten up with worry, and you ain't going to rest until I'm the same way."

Micah and Elbert went inside the saloon ordered glasses of watered down whiskey and a bucket of flat, warm beer that they drank using their own tin coffee cups. One of the saloon girls caught Micah's eye. She had dark raven hair and wore a modest blue calico day dress.

Three dusty drovers surrounded her. Two were Anglos, and the third a Tejano, and they still wore their leather *chaparreras*. Such men were skilled riders and their tanned skins were toughened by sun and wind and their work. They seemed indifferent to the soldiers about them, to the talk of war filling the room, to even the importance of their own work to the cause of the Confederacy. The South was hungrier with every year of the war, and Texas cattle were an important source of food. The girl laughed at something one of the drovers said and she tossed her hair. She caught Micah's eye and smiled bashfully.

"Damnation," Micah said. "She sure is a pretty thing."

"I think she cottons to you, Micah," Elbert said.

"She's a hussy. She'd cotton to anyone who would pay her."

"You going to pay her?"

"Likely not. I've got Erin to think about. I swore to her that I'd behave myself around other women."

Elbert drained the glass of whiskey and chased it down with a sip of beer. "I'm married too, but it ain't going to stop me from going to that whorehouse next door. Doing without a woman makes a man not think right, and we ain't been near a woman in months."

One of the soldiers called out for the girl to sing "Lorena." She was young, and yet when she sang, Micah detected a voice that held years of passion and suffering beyond her age. She got some of the notes wrong, but Micah received some comfort from her voice anyway.

Elbert set down his cup of beer and stood up. "Well, I reckon I'll see you sometime before morning." He lifted the tin bucket of beer. "You done with this?" Without waiting for Micah's reply, he went to the cowhands and set it on their table.

"You boys look thirsty. Can't abide the thought of seeing a fellow Texan thirsty."

"Much obliged," one of the cowhands said.

"I think we'll take you up on that. It's been a long trip. We're dry," one of the drovers said. "Days and days of looking at nothing but these ornery cows makes a man thirsty for whiskey and women."

Elbert motioned the girl over with his hand. "My lonely friend over yonder took a liking to your singing. Micah said he'd pay you to sit with him a bit. He's a timid sort or he would have asked you himself. I think he needs some cheering up."

2

The girl left the cowboys and walked to Micah's table. She sat next to Micah and after they had drank and talked a while, she led him into a back room. After they undressed, he clutched her tightly, savoring the warmth and softness of her slender body. Her skin was clean and smelled of rosewater. As he kissed and touched her, his mind moved to thoughts of a spring three years ago and a field of bluebonnets and the girl with the blue-bonnet eyes. He whispered, "Erin, you are so beautiful . . . "

"My name is Mary," the girl whispered, "but tonight I'll be anyone you want me to be."

Micah woke from his reverie and pushed the girl away. "I don't want you to be nobody for me." He reached for his haversack, dug into it, and pitched her a dollar. "Get dressed and get your skinny ass out of here."

"This is my room," Mary said. "So, I think you should leave instead."

\*\*\*

Micah left the girl's crib and returned to the saloon. Elbert was not in sight. Most of the soiled doves were absent as well, but the tavern was still full of soldiers and drovers. Micah dragged a stool to the wall. He set his hat in his lap, slicked back his hair with his hand and leaned back against the oak boards. He blew out his breath and said out loud, "If you ain't a sight, Micah."

"Damned, if we ain't all a sight."

Micah turned to the voice. A soldier sat alone at the table next to him. He wore the uniform common to men in the Army of the Trans-Mississippi--a gray kepi, a brown-gray sack coat and trousers that looked to have once been sky blue like the Federal soldiers wore. A rifle, wrapped in a quilt, lay on the table in front of him.

"Yes, Lord, ain't we a site," the man said again. He emptied his glass of whiskey and slammed it down on the table.

"You've had a bad night, I guess," Micah said.

"I've had two months of bad nights."

"Mine hasn't exactly turned out like I imagined," Micah said.

"Well, if we're going to drink and talk the rest of the god-awful night, you might as well drag that wobbly stool to this table. What brings you to Fort Worth?"

Micah set the stool closer to the man and dropped his hat on the table. "We're on furlough after Mansfield. Dropped off some Federal prisoners at Camp Ford in Tyler."

"Yeah, we sure gave the Yankees a drubbing at Mansfield, didn't we. Could you stand another drink?" the man asked. Without waiting for Micah's reply, he walked to the bar and returned with two schooners of beer. "You can call me Silas, if you care to call me anything. Drink up. And your name, sir?" He slid the glass of beer towards Micah.

Micah lifted his glass in a salute. "Much obliged. I'm Micah Evans."

"I saw you go out with that woman," Silas said. "You came back mighty quick. I figure either you were either in a hurry or you changed your mind about doing such things."

"I changed my mind. I ain't no whoremonger."

The soldier nodded and his hand stroked the grizzled stubble on his chin. "I've changed my mind every night. Still on the straight and narrow, but I am not sure how long that will last."

The man drank deeply from the schooner and wiped the foam from his mouth with his sleeve. "I need to clean myself up, but I can't seem to drag myself out of this place. I've been drinking steadily three days now. Haven't left except to go to the shithouse. Passed out on my way back one time. I'm about out of steam." He took another drink. "Yes, sir, about out of steam."

"What put you on this drunk?" Micah said.

"A hard question that is, Micah. A question that many men, including myself, have asked, and wrestled with on many a night. But the answer—that's what's really hard, but if I drink enough, the answer is hard to remember."

"I don't quite get the point of what you're saying," Micah said.

"I signed on with the 17th Alabama Sharpshooters. I was given a roving commission as an independent sharpshooter and scout. I could go where I please, and wage war at my own sweet will. Our company

4

was one of those units attached to different brigades according to the whims of high command. Sometimes they only attach one of us—as in my case. Some idiot sent me to General Kirby in Shreveport. Only he didn't know nothing about my orders, and he doesn't care for sharpshooters particularly. He says that climbing trees and shooting men at long distances doesn't seem civilized. Civilized . . . That was the word he used. There isn't anything civilized about this war we're in. Maybe there should be, but there isn't. So, after sitting in Shreveport for a week someone made me a courier and sent me with a message to take to General Henry McCullough, only he ain't here. They say he's established his headquarters in Bonham. My horse is lame, and I'll probably drink myself to death before the ignorant fools in charge get me another or decide what they're going to do with me."

"Must be discouraging," Micah said.

"It is. But ennui and frustration with military intelligence is not what has created this black cloud of depression I carry on my heart and soul. Mine is a burden I've resolved and resigned myself to carry till I'm in my grave. Do you have a family, Micah Evans?"

"My wife, Erin, and a set of twins in Jack County. I haven't seen them in two years. I should be there instead of here."

"You should indeed. Jack County. I hear the savages are running wild there these days, killing, looting. If I were you, I'd get home and bring those loved ones closer to civilization. Let me tell you a story, Micah Evans. The last time I was in Alabama, I found the Yankees had burned my house. I couldn't find my wife, and nearly lost my mind. Then I finally found her at a relative's homeplace, and I surely did lose my senses. My cousin's family had found her wandering the roads. The Yankees had abused her so terribly that she was addled." He clenched his teeth and hissed, "She didn't even know who I was. I didn't know what else to do, so I left her in my cousin's care and went on to Shreveport as ordered.

"Go home, Micah. Go home to your wife and twins. You won't regret going home, and if you do return, you can shed that guilty conscience and worry that's written on your face."

"I am going home. I should get there late tomorrow." Micah looked at the quilt-wrapped rifle. "A Kerr?"

"No, a Whitworth." Silas unwrapped the scoped rifle, lifted it by the stock, and handed it to Micah. "An English rifle. Ever seen one?"

"Nope, but it looks like a fine piece. What's the caliber? Appears to be rather small."

Silas dropped a three-inch, hexagonal piece of lead on the table. " It shoots a.45 caliber bolt. Most accurate rifle in the South. One like this one killed a Yankee general at Chickamauga at 1,000 yards. It's been rumored his last words were 'They couldn't hit an elephant at this range.' Some other sharpshooters have killed Yankees at 1500 yards."

Micah computed the distance. "That's a far piece." He thought of how handy the rifle would have been when he was a Ranger. The Comanches always managed to stay just out of range of their rifles, flaunting Texan scalps hanging from their lances and mocking the Rangers' impotent helplessness. Micah handed the rifle back to him. "You reckon you'll go back to Alabama?"

"What for? What's there for me? For anyone? Nothing but chimneys of burned-out homes left by Sherman's Mongols. Anyway, I seem to have lost all my gumption. Likely I'll just stay here and drink myself blind and senseless." He drained the last of his beer. "My mind is numb, my tongue thick from drink, and still the terrors of the heart afflict me so. I'm no weak man, Micah Evans, but I was not prepared for the suffering God has thrust upon me. How can a sorry sample of humanity like myself be allowed to live, and my Rosie . . . My poor Rosie . . . ." Silas withdrew a single-shot shotgun pistol from his belt, set in on the table and spun it. The worn barrel passed Micah and wobbled to a stop in front of its owner, pointing at him like the needle of a compass. "Bang!" he said.

"You best be careful playing with a loaded pistol like that," Micah said. "They've been known to be temperamental and unstable at times."

"Just like people," he replied. Silas stood up and slipped the pistol into his belt. "You're a good man, Micah Evans. Go home, while you still have one to go to. Go before the damn Kiowa or Comanche or Kansas jayhawkers take your home away. I'm headed toward the shithouse, and I leave my rifle and gear in your care and under your watchful eye." He dropped some coins on the table. "Buy us two drinks if you would."

Micah had sat down with the two glasses of whisky on the table, when he heard the blast of the shotgun pistol. He slowly drank down one glass of whisky. He lifted the other and said, "To you, Silas." He reached his hand into the soldier's haversack and withdrew a small leather-framed daguerreotype. Opening it, he saw an image of the soldier's wife and sweetheart. He studied the dark curls and sparkling eyes of this woman who had been a man's religion until men in blue had ravaged her and by that savage act had destroyed heart, hearth, and heroism in one vicious swoop. The girl was still alive, but no longer on *terra firma*, she was on this earth, but no longer of it. Silas had lost her forever. Micah thought about the men who had violated her. Such men were more than undisciplined—they were barbarians so sunk into cruelty that they had severed the bonds of decency and civilized behavior. Wild dogs of men set on the civilians of the South. These thoughts churned Micah's insides.

Micah slung the man's cartridge pouch and haversack on his shoulder and picked up the quilt-wrapped rifle. He found Silas behind the saloon. Micah pried the pistol from his hand and replaced it with the photograph of the girl. He draped the bloody head with its kepi and said, "Now you and your lass are together, Silas."

Micah looked up at the moon, draping the body of Silas with its light like a burial shroud, then turned and returned to the saloon. He would find Elbert somehow and they would leave for Jack County tonight. And once he got there, he knew he'd never leave his family again.

# The Heart Is Not Made of Bone—Krio Proverb

I was sent to Freetown, Sierra Leone by the *Dallas Morning News* to write a story on the nation's recovery after its bloody civil war. One night I went to Paddy's Bar and Chinese Restaurant. Paddy's was a favorite haunt of Westerners and had a reputation for being a place where Africa met the world. The food was good, the drinks affordable, and usually patrons crowded the bar to capacity. I had made an appointment to meet with Father Ambrose, a priest whose mission and village in the northern district was overrun by RUF soldiers. I knew it would not be a pretty story—there were no pretty stories coming out of Sierra Leone—but I hoped it would give me insight into the soul and hearts of the nation's people. My first question was: "What is the most important truth you've learned from your experience?" He sipped on his Scotch, then answered: "I learned that the heart is not made of bone." Father Ambrose and I talked and drank long into the night. His bandaged right hand rested on the bar, a reminder of a night he and many others would never forget. Here is the story he gave me that I submitted to my editor. It was never published.

## A Priest's Tale: Machetes and Words

If it weren't for the AK 47's they carried, the Zebra Small Boys Battalion would have appeared to be an African version of the Boy Scouts out for an afternoon stroll, dressed in a collage of fatigues and American T-shirts and jeans. Their hands and clothes were spotted and crusted with the blood of those newly slain or violated. The soldiers surrounded a small herd of captives like malignant spectres. A line of porters, even younger than the soldiers, trailed behind them, and they were loaded down with the looted goods of Kamakwie and Kamalu.

As the invaders entered the mission compound in the Northern District of Sierra Leone, Father Ambrose contemplated the scene. Many of the villagers were terrified. The screams, weeping, moans, and prayers blended together into a demented chorus, and the sounds of the choir's grief and terror burned and burrowed into his soul.

In the eyes and faces of the soldiers, he recognized the signs of drug madness and bloodlust. He whispered to Sister Agnes, "Calm the villagers. Tell them they must stop the wailing. It will only feed the soldiers' rage and frenzy. Find out what has happened in Kamalu. Minister to any wounded the best you can without attracting attention."

"I will, father. May God help us," Sister Agnes said. As she tended to the terrified villagers, the priest counted twenty boy-soldiers. Two older soldiers hung in the background. One was white, the other mulatto. The aloofness of the two older men suggested they were either mercenaries or senior RUF officers.

One of the boy soldiers sauntered to the truck and barked a command. All the soldiers dropped their prizes and snapped to attention. He spoke again and pointed, and a soldier set a wooden rocker upon a stack of wooden crates.

A teenager with a Machiavellian smile, he slowly scanned the eyes of villagers and the young soldiers. He clambered up the boxes and sat on the improvised throne, impatiently drumming his fingers on the chair's arm. A soldier rolled a stump to a spot directly in front of the prisoners. The enthroned one spoke dramatically, as if he made an important speech.

Father Ambrose couldn't understand the young boy-leader. He thought the dialect might be Mende. He stepped forward.

"I don't understand you, my son," he said. He addressed the two older soldiers. "Do any of you speak English? Or Temne? Is he your leader? Why does he not speak Krio?"

The white soldier held his hand up, palm toward the boy-leader and caught his attention. The white soldier motioned toward the priest and said in Krio, "The priest-man, he wants to know who you are and what you want. Can I tell him?"

"Tell him," the boy said in English, and then continued speaking in the unknown tongue.

The white man stepped closer to the priest and translated: "The General prefers to address his audience in Mende. He understands some English, and Krio of course, but it makes him feel more important to be translated. God, these black buggers I work with are vain. I'll tell you what he says, priest. He says, 'I am General Share Blood.' He greets you warmly. He says, 'We are soldiers of the Revolutionary United Front. At Papa's orders, we are here to liberate you from the corrupt government in Freetown. I have been told that you warn your Christians to not join Papa's Army. Why? Is this a sign that you mean to betray us? You must learn you cannot show such disrespect.' "

General Share Blood pointed to two Kamalu boys.

The white soldier left the priest and yanked two boys away from their parents. Father Ambrose thought that neither boy could be over ten years of age. The white soldier cocked his AK 47 and thrust it into one boy's hands, pointed to the other who was less than five feet away, and said, "Kill him."

The victim pleaded, "Please, I know you. Do not kill me!"

The mercenary slapped the boy's head. "Do it now!"

The boy pulled the trigger.

"That's a good soldier. *Gud pikin.*" The white soldier snatched his rifle from the boy's trembling hands and shoved him toward the other soldiers. "Sit down."

Father Ambrose bowed his head and prayed for murdered and murderer. This action had forever separated the young boy from the village of Kamalu. The new recruit could never come home.

General Share Blood pointed to Father Ambrose. "You have diamonds for me?"

"No," Father Ambrose said. "We have no diamonds. All of the diamond mines are far from here."

"You do not speak true. You have diamonds." He clapped his hands three times.

The boy soldiers herded another group of villagers forward and gunned them down. The slaughter was followed by an ecstatic dance around the bodies. As they danced, the drunken and drugged executioners howled and fired their guns wildly into the air.

"Now you have diamonds for me?" General Share Blood asked.

Father Ambrose feared the mission staff might be killed next. He once again attempted to communicate. "I tell you we have no diamonds. This is cattle country." Father Ambrose called out to the white man, "Who are you? Why are you here with these boys? Are you a mercenary? Are you not a high-ranking officer? Do you not see what they have just done? You must order him to stop this senseless killing. These people have done nothing to harm or threaten you. Have you no conscience?"

The white man sat down in front of Ambrose. "No, I don't." He dropped a box of cartridges on the ground in front of him, and slowly reloaded his rifle magazine. The box was covered with Arabic writing.

"Conscience is a luxury I cannot afford," the white man replied. "I 'm here as an advisor. About what's happened——I don't try to make sense of these buggers' politics."

General Share Blood stood and stretched lazily, then resumed his seat. "It is time for the games," he said in English. He drained a gourd of palm wine, then looked down upon the throng before him as if he were indeed perched on a royal throne. "I am thirsty for my daily drink of blood. Who among you will provide it? Perhaps you?" General Share Blood pointed at Brother Thomas.

One soldier in a Rambo T-shirt grabbed the mission's gardener by the shirt collar and dragged him forward. The gardener's little girl clung to his leg screaming. Brother Thomas tried to pry loose his little girl's hands, but she clung stubbornly. When Brother Thomas and his daughter in tow reached the stump in front of General Share Blood, the Rambo soldier placed the man's arm across the top of the stump and drew his machete.

As he raised the blade, Father Ambrose stepped forward and placed his hand on the young soldier's shoulder. "No, my son. Do not hurt this man. He is good man, good friend."

The soldier holding the gardener squinted at the priest through cocaine and ganja-glazed eyes. He glanced at the general, then back to the priest. Something human etched itself upon his face.

"Father, I do not know what I do," he whispered.

"Put the cutlass down, my son," Father Ambrose said quietly. "You are a Christian man. I know you are afraid, but God will give you strength."

The trembling blade rose for a moment, then the young soldier stabbed the machete into the earth, and knelt before the priest with his eyes to the ground.

Some of the soldiers hooted and laughed. General Share Blood shouted for the soldier to continue.

"No," the young Rambo replied. "I will not hurt this man." Then to Father Ambrose he whispered, "Bless me, Father, for I have sinned."

Father Ambrose knelt and gave the repentant man absolution in an abbreviated form, confident that God would accept the adaptation.

General Blood's retort was sharp, and two soldiers dragged the rebellious Rambo forward and held him before the General. After the General clumsily climbed down from his wooden-box throne, he plucked a long, dry leaf from a nearby tree, and rolled it up like a cigar. He lit it with a cigarette lighter, then as his troops held the man's face, pressed the burning leaf into the soldier's eye.

General Blood smiled at the soldier's screams. He swaggered around, looking at his soldiers and his captives, holding a fist in the air triumphantly.

Father Ambrose stood and shouted, "Listen to me, all of you!" He looked at the white mercenary. "Please, do not let him do this. Ask your leader to take what he wants, but please, do not injure anyone else. We will not assist any of your enemies. "

He was cut short when the mercenary barked a command and one of the soldiers pushed him roughly to the ground. The mercenary slung his rifle onto his shoulder and strode toward the priest. On his way he kicked the sobbing young boy-soldier who was clutching his eye and writhing on the ground like a wounded snake.

"That's the problem when you don't take them young enough," the mercenary said. "I thought he was going to make a fine soldier, but I guess I was wrong. Our training was wasted on him. Now, if he lives, he won't even be fit to be a porter."

"You do not talk like a man should, but like an animal," Father Ambrose said. "No wonder the people of Salone fear and hate your soldiers. The RUF once were men of ideals who talked of helping the people of Salone. But now . . ."

The mercenary knelt and whispered, "Priest, I tend to like men in your occupation, but we don't have time for a long philosophical discussion. The situation is actually very simple. The towns of this district and your mission are now under the control of the RUF. The ideals you speak of left Salone with the educated elite émigrés, and the same ideals left the RUF when Papa discovered how much money he could make in the diamond trade. Now, you cooperate and I might get you out of this in one piece. I want you to hook up your radio and call whomever you need to call and have them send money and diamonds. The general wants diamonds; but he and I both will settle for American dollars. Then, maybe he will let you go."

"Diamonds? He wants blood diamonds?" Father Ambrose felt a rage coursing through his body and he surrendered to it. He shouted, "And you want money? You want us to ask for ransom? You white devil! You want me to cooperate with this sadist and ask for money to buy our freedom? No!"

The mercenary patted Father Ambrose's face, turned to General Share Blood and in Krio said, "The priest, he will not respect the General."

Shouting, the General leaped from the chair to the ground.

Father Ambrose felt boys' hands clutching and dragging him forward. He was thrown to the ground next to the mission's gardener and his daughter, and the three of the knelt together before General Share Blood.

Ambrose looked up into the face of a young girl beside the general. She drew a machete from her web belt and nodded toward Brother Thomas, the gardener. Two soldiers stretched Thomas's arm across the stump, and with a deft stroke, she amputated his right hand. Then she pointed to the little girl. Two strokes this time. The girl swooned and fell to her knees, a Lavinia holding up two bleeding handless limbs.

At the sight, the priest felt his heart break within himself, and he knew now that all the sadness he had ever felt and all the evil and suffering he had ever seen had reached a culminating point, a climax. As if in the audience of a tragic play, he waited for the drama's catharsis, the purging of his heart through pity and terror.

The machete-wielding girl smiled and pointed to Father Ambrose.

Father Ambrose felt the rough top of the stump against his skin, felt the wetness of Thomas's blood underneath, saw the whiteness of his own skin in the fading light.

General Share Blood held the mission's gold communion cup in his hands. The general turned dramatically, displaying the chalice to the group. He handed it to one soldier who knelt in front of the stump and held it at the ready. Father Ambrose flexed his fingers, staring at his hand.

What followed seemed to happen in slow motion. A machete flashes in the fading sunlight. He hears a thwack, a thumping sound. The fingers wriggle on his detached left hand, convulsing on top of the stump as if they now had a life of their own apart from his brain. The hand rolls to the ground with the other three hands where it seems to crawl about. Another boy lifts the priest's arm so the blood drips into the communion cup. His heart pumps four times and the cup is full. White hands wrap coarse twine tightly around his arm to stem the bleeding.

The foaming cup is placed reverently into General Share Blood's hands. Father Ambrose stared at the smooth, flat wall of bone and nerves and tissue where his hand used to be. The thought was odd, but he thanked God the machete used was sharp. He had heard tales of how the machetes were often dull and how they mangled the limbs of victims. Ambrose remained on his knees. He knew his body was in shock, but he couldn't think of what he should do or say about it.

He glanced up into the smiling, drugged face of the machete-girl. He studied her blood-splotched face as if it were an icon of a black Madonna. *An amazon*, Father Ambrose thought. *This girl is a true amazon. She would amputate anything, even her own breast if it were in her way.* He heard her chatter to the others in Krio. He felt a strong hand on his shoulder, and he turned. Another icon. This time, it is the tear-stained face of Sister Agnes. "What is she saying?" he asked her. "The machete-girl there."

Sister Agnes drew him to her bosom. Her breast felt soft, warm, comforting. "She calls herself Betty Cut Hands and she is General Shareblood's queen. Here, open your mouth." She pressed two tablets onto his tongue. "Swallow them. They're pain pills. We have no water, so you'll have to swallow them dry. Now, close your eyes. I'm sure you are in shock."

He swallowed the pills but he didn't close his eyes. From within her embrace, he watched as drugs were mixed into the communion cup holding his blood and stirred with the General's finger. The General, still thirsty for his daily blood, drank the priest's blood and thumped his chest with his fist. He pointed to other soldiers who one by one came to the altar of the stump to sup and share in the sacred ritual of his perverted communion. The chalice was returned to the General and after he drained it, he set it on a crate next to him. He licked his lips, and his eyes rolled with delight.

Father Ambrose turned his head and wept. Through the veil of tears, he spotted Tejan. How long had it been since that terrible day when the RUF kidnapped Tejan and five other students? Four years? Tejan possessed the same glazed eyes as the others, and an AK 47 was slung over his shoulder.

Father Ambrose tried to focus his blurred, swirling vision. He raised himself and rubbed at his burning eyes with the stump of his right hand. He attempted to stand and go to Tejan, but the world spun in a strange mosaic of black and white faces, and he collapsed backwards into Sister Agnes's arms.

"Father, here, I will wipe your eyes," Sister Agnes whispered. "What can I do? What will happen with us?"

He willed himself to answer her, but his tongue was thick and slow. Finally, he uttered, *"Vado mori."* He buried his face in her bosom. It was time to leave this sad earth. He knew too much now, had seen too much.

"No, Father," she whispered. "You cannot die and leave us alone."

When he woke, he was still alive in the sister's arms. Everything of value in the mission and village had been piled in front of General Share Blood, who had returned to his throne of boxes. The priest's hand was now buried beneath a pile of black hands, arms, legs, and ears. Several buildings and houses about them were burning. From within one he heard screams and saw black arms reaching out from the flames like anguished souls trapped in a torture chamber of hell.

The General's soldiers had found more palm wine. As they drained gourd after gourd, they fired their guns into the air, and they danced and staggered about a large fire like stiff skeletons in a *danse macbre*. One soldier had donned a nun's habit, another a choir robe. Father Ambrose watched the one-eyed, disobedient soldier embrace a palm tree and struggle to pull himself to his feet. When he finally wrestled himself upright, a machine gun riddled his body and he died with his one good eye open, his arms still clutching the palm.

Father Ambrose thought the RUF soldiers had executed the one-eyed soldier until he saw the mulatto fall. Then General Share Blood and his chair throne tumbled backwards. When the general's body hit the ground, the gold communion cup bounced toward the priest. There was no blood in the chalice. Several of the dancing boy-soldiers dropped one by one as they too were splattered with bullets. An enemy presence was perceived and the boy soldiers of the Zebra battalion broke and ran.

The white mercenary stood his ground, methodically taking aim and firing his automatic rifle. Bullets peppered his white skin, and he fell to his knees. Then when a bullet struck his forehead, he fell face-first to the dark ground. A group of black shadows swarmed him, and Ambrose heard the sound of the clubs and spears as they struck and tore at his corpse.

Several men sprinted past Father Ambrose in pursuit of the fleeing Zebra battalion. Some of the men were in fatigues, and others wore animal skins. One pushed Ambrose to the ground.

"We have come to help you, Fader," he said. " Please, you are to stay close to de ground."

"Father?" Sister Agnes whispered as she ducked down next to him. "What's happening?"

"Government soldiers and Kamajors," he said. "And maybe some Nigerian troops from Makeni. Stay down until we're sure it's safe."

"Oh, thank God they have come," she whispered.

A Kamajor threw a Zebra boy down near them and then machined-gunned him. The young rebel's body bounced like a martinet as the bullets riddled his adolescent body. The Kamajor looked down at Ambrose and smiled. "It be OK soon, Fader," he said. "Good Christians be here now."

Father Ambrose turned his head from the sight of the boy's body. "Yes, Sister Agnes," he said. "Thank God they have come."

The Kamajors and soldiers returned from their pursuit, herding several of the Zebra boys in front of them, caning them unmercifully every step. The mission captives watched as the Kamajors beat and then executed the rebels one by one with their guns or staves. A few of the younger rebel boys were terrified and began to moan senselessly, as if they were deaf and dumb. But the ruse of being a handicapped child was unconvincing, and the beatings and executions continued. The wails of the boy-soldiers filled the night and the sound could have been the audio illustration for the nightmarish paintings of Munch or Goya.

Two more Kamajors returned, dragging a body. Father Ambrose saw that it was Tejan, a boy who had been taken from the village two years ago. The priest watched as they kicked him and whipped him with sticks. When one pointed a rifle at his head, Father Ambrose shouted, "No! He is one of ours!"

"Are you sure, Fader?" the Kamajor said. "He look like rebel soldier moment ago. He fight me hard with his empty gun before I conk him on de head."

"I am sure. His name is Tejan," he said. With his right hand, he picked up the gold communion cup and held it out to the Kamajor. "He's probably just frightened."

"You can have him, Fader." The Kamajor stuffed the chalice into his fanny pack and moved on.

"Father!" Sister Agnes whispered. "What are you doing? This boy probably did some horrible things to . . . ."

"Hush, sister. The sin will be on my own soul. I knew this boy and his parents, and, demon though he is now, I'm not going to give him up to these murderers. He was kidnapped by the RUF a few years ago. Now, help me with him."

Together, they dragged the unconscious Tejan over to their group. Fortunately, Tejan had not been shot, only clubbed. A cane had laid his head open, and Sister Agnes pressed her hand on the wound.

"Tejan . . . Tejan . . . Do you know who I am?" Ambrose asked.

Tejan's eyes opened, and he groaned.

Several villagers shook their heads in disgust at the priest. Ambrose knew they perceived his mercy as another example of the strange behavior and values of the *poo-muis* and that it confirmed their long-held suspicions of the priest-man's naiveté.

The Kamajors and government troops moved on in their search for more rebels. When the mission staff had buried the dead and every body part they could find, they filled the mission's Toyota truck with the weak and wounded, twenty-three in all, and began the drive to Freetown. There they would join thousands of other refugees seeking safety and peace. Eventually, the RUF was defeated, some semblance of peace was restored, but nightmares are slow to fade in this land that few Americans know anything about.

\*\*\*

From that sad priest I heard a story, a dark one of suffering, of one boy's redemption, and of a priest who had nearly lost his faith. I learned that many reporters had covered those war days, the days of the Blood Diamonds, and written stories that were never published in our news. Some reporters, like many religious leaders, had paid with their lives. The suffering of Sierra Leone in those years is almost more than one can absorb. There is a glimmer of hope for the future, but nothing is for certain. The priest's story would never leave my mind. Sometimes I wake from a dream in which it is my hand that is lost, and I feel that ache in my heart that reminds me that truly, the heart is not made of bone.

# The Lost Bazaar

"The art of our necessities is strange . . ."

--*King Lear*

On New Year's Eve, Larry drifted slowly down Trenton Street in West Monroe, Louisiana, warming his hands in the side pockets of his faded olive-green field jacket. Pausing in front of each store window, he studied the antique furniture and other goods on display. When he came to an art gallery, his eyes were drawn to a wooden sign above him that read: WELCOME TO THE LOST BAZAAR. Suspended by chains, the sign rocked whenever a gust of wind nudged it, rasping despondent creaks and groans in the gaps of silence between passing cars. A cardboard placard was taped to the glass of an ancient wooden door. Larry moved his index finger across the page word by word:

> ARTISTS: WE WILL REPRESENT AND SELL YOUR WORK ON COMMISSION. NORTHEAST LOUISIANA IS INVITED TO ATTEND OUR NEW YEAR'S DAY RECEPTION. THIS YEAR'S FEATURED ARTIST: DELIA JOHNSON.

The gallery was closed. Larry took off his ball cap and pressed his face to the smudged, tinted glass and peered at several paintings hanging inside on the plaster walls. Adjacent to the window stood a bronze sculpture of a naked man with raised fists and empty eye sockets. His mouth was opened wide as if he were tortured and howling in rage or dementia. Next to this simulacrum stood another bronze figure of a kneeling nude young woman who held her hands to her face as if she wept for the man's anguish. Larry rubbed his burning eyes.

"Now, we see through a glass darkly . . ."

For a moment, Larry thought the man-statue had spoken. He shook his head. When he heard a snicker, he turned and saw a man peering over his shoulder. The man clutched a scuffed duffel bag in one hand and with the other he touched his face as a man does when he inspects himself before a mirror when shaving. He wore a pointed stocking cap that was pulled down to his thick black eyebrows. His dark eyes were big and wild, and he grinned, revealing teeth that were stained and crooked.

"What?" Larry said.

The man pointed at the statues. "Dress them up in a few clothes and they might look human."

"I guess."

"I reckon this must be some kind of museum."

"An art gallery actually."

"Well, I'll be. I wonder what else they got on display inside. I used to be a preacher, showing people the way to that great art gallery in the sky. In fact, folks just generally call me, Preacher. That's because I quote the Bible so much."

"Glad to meet you, Preacher. My name's Larry."

"You remind me of an uncle of mine. He had a coat like that too. Served in Viet Nam he did. He blew his brains out though. You know what time it is?"

"I sold my watch a couple of weeks ago. I do know it's New Year's Eve."

"That's close enough. The exact time don't matter much noway. I came in from Mississippi on the train. You?"

"Walked and hitchhiked here. I've been out West. Mostly rambling through Texas."

"Ah, you are a true King of the Road, a pilgrim walking till he reaches that better land!"

"Where are you headed?" Larry asked.

"I don't know, my fellow vagabond, but I reckon I'll get there somehow. King Larry, could you spare some change to help a man get a drink?"

"Sure. I got a few bucks, and could use a drink myself. I don't have much, but I'm glad to share what I got."

"Like the Bible says, give strong drink unto him that is ready to perish," Preacher said, "and wine unto those that be of heavy hearts. Let him drink, and forget his poverty, and remember his misery no more."

"Are you sure the Bible says that?"

"It does for a fact. Speaks right to the heart, don't it."

"There's a ring of truth to it," Larry said.

Preacher pointed toward the river. "Round the bend yonder I saw a bar. We could go there."

"Sure. It's bound to be warmer and drier than standing here."

They crossed Trenton Street and walked toward the river. As they walked, Preacher sang, "Little Brown Jug."

Larry looked up at the sky. The gray clouds were thick with moisture. South of town, large plumes of smoke billowed up into the sky from a paper mill's concrete smokestacks. The north wind gnawed its way through his jacket, and the light mist, which earlier floated and drifted to the ground, changed to a driving rain and sleet that pelted and stung Larry's face.

"I never can get used to walking in the rain," Larry said. "I hate it."

"The good Lord makes his rain fall on the just and the unjust."

"I still don't like it."

Near the levee they passed through an opening in a concrete block floodwall and sloshed through the parking lot to the Cottonport Lounge. Larry paused outside the door and studied the Ouachita River and the reflections of buildings and lights shimmering on the dark water's surface.

"We're going down the river one by one," Preacher said.

"You must be a hoot at funerals," Larry said. "You probably have a Bible verse ready for every occasion."

"I do indeed. How much money you got, King Larry? The Bible says 'money answers all things.'"

"Five dollars." Larry scraped the bottoms of his muddy boots on the edge of the concrete porch.

"Tain't much for us to drink on," Preacher said.

"Sorry. It's all I got. Look for unfinished drinks. Shoot them down and no one will be the wiser. Let's go on inside."

They entered and sat down at an empty table near the door. Larry stretched out his cramped legs and felt drafts of heated air push the cold dampness of his jeans against his skin. He leaned his head against the wall and closed his eyes and thought of last week's walk through the West Texas Badlands and how the wind had pushed him relentlessly out of Texas into Louisiana.

A waitress came to their table. "What would you men like to drink tonight?"

Larry opened his eyes. "Let me have a Budweiser."

She nodded toward Preacher. "What'll he have?"

"A glass of red wine," Preacher said, "for my stomach's sake." He snickered.

The waitress rolled her eyes, took Larry's money, and returned with their drinks.

"You got any free snacks?" Preacher asked. "I'm a mite bit hungry."

"We'll have some *hors d'oeuvres* laid out later for the New Year's Eve party," she said.

"Thank you, cupbearer," Preacher said. "I was hungry and you gave me meat." He gulped down his wine.

"Don't drink so fast," Larry said. "The longer your drink lasts, the less they'll hustle you to buy more."

"Ah, wine that maketh glad the heart of man!" Preacher said. "The Lord shall provide more, King Larry."

Larry sipped his beer slowly and studied the motley crowd. The image reminded him of a bar scene in *Star Wars*. A menagerie of alien humans milled about him in various stages of drunkenness—mutants, weirdoes, rednecks, and deviants in mismatched or bizarre clothes. A bartender in a tuxedo jabbered with a man in a leisure suit. A plump brunette wearing a plastic tiara and a short black sequined dress brayed to her friends with a high-pitched voice. One man sported a heavily bearded face and a bandoleer of wine coolers across his chest. He grunted with each step as he strutted past their table.

"Hey, it's Chewbacca!" Larry whispered.

"Watch this, King Larry," Preacher said. "Hey, fool!" he shouted.

Three men at the bar turned and looked at him.

"No, not none of you," Preacher said. He pointed toward the back of the lounge. "Way back there." He snickered when they looked that direction.

"I think I'm gonna mingle with the church," Preacher said. "You know, check on the indwelling of the spirits." He left the table and walked through the bar, talking to various people as if they were lost and delinquent members of his lost congregation. His arms flapped wildly as he bellowed out strange Bible verses. Soon, one man went to the bar and fetched Preacher a bottle of wine.

"Yes, sir," Preacher predicated. "A man's gotta be baptized and warsh away his past sins. That old man's gotta die and be buried in the water before a new one can rise up. Course, baptism don't always take if'n you don't do it right."

A slender redheaded woman entered the Cottonport. She wore a gray crewneck sweater and blue jeans. Her pale slender fingers wiped rain from her freckled face then nervously tapped her leg. She scanned the bar and when her eyes fell on Larry, she smiled.

"Looking for someone?" Larry asked. For a second, Larry thought he knew her, but then dismissed the idea as wishful thinking.

"My friends, but I don't see them. I guess I need to find a table and save them seats."

"You're welcome to take this one. I'll move to the bar." Larry pushed back his chair to get up.

She sat in Preacher's chair. "I'll take a seat, but you don't have to leave. It's sweet of you to offer me your table though."

The band began a song by John Prine.

"Oh, I know this song!" she said.

Larry found himself listening to the words—something about how fast the sound of loneliness can be.

"My name's Larry," he said.

"I'm Delia."

"Ready for the New Year?" Larry asked.

"Yeah, ready for a better one. It's got to be a better one or I don't know what I'll do."

"I know the feeling."

"Damn. Here I am again in West Monroe on New Year's Eve," she said. "Most of my life I've waited around this piss-pot town hoping for things to be different. But they never are." She looked at his face. "Your eyes are awfully red. Do they hurt?"

"No more than usual."

Preacher was perched on a pool table, wolfing down sandwiches and guzzling wine. He set down his glass and beckoned Larry to come to him.

"Excuse me a minute," Larry said. "I must consult with my philosopher."

"What?"

"Nothing. Just trying to make a joke."

Larry walked over to Preacher. "What do you want?"

"There is a time to dance," Preacher said, then with his hand dismissed him.

Larry grinned and returned to Delia just as the band began a slow song. He slipped off his field jacket and draped it across his chair. "Hey, dance with me, lady."

"Sure."

They danced in small circular movements on the crowded dance floor. Delia gently laid her head on his shoulder and sighed. "This is nice. It's been a while."

Preacher waved a paper horn at them as if it were a wand, as if he were bestowing a blessing upon them.

"Look at that lunatic friend of yours," she said.

"Aw, he's alright. We're probably all crazy in one way or another. It's easy to do, to go crazy."

"Yeah, it is. I've been on the edge a few times myself. What do you do, Larry?"

"I travel."

"Are you in sales or something?"

"No. I'm gainfully unemployed right now."

"Do you just drive your car from place to place?"

"I don't have a car."

"Well, how do you travel if you don't have a car?"

"I either hitchhike or walk mostly. I have hopped a train or two, but I don't like traveling in boxcars. Rough company, and the trains don't run on schedule anymore. Everything's so damned unpredictable these days—the weather, jobs, trains, people."

"Where will you go next?"

"I don't know. Any suggestions?"

"Are you like homeless or something?" she asked.

"Only by choice, till I get my head together."

"How sad. But you don't look or sound like a homeless person to me. How did you end up like this?"

"I just left one day. Got sick of the way things were, so I just left. Should have done it years ago, but I've always held on to things longer than I should. It's not too bad. I find an odd job now and then, sleep where I can, then I walk somewhere else. I don't know why I'm telling you this crap. Let's talk about something else. What do you do?"

"I work for State Farm."

"Selling insurance?" he asked.

"No, I work in the administrative offices. I hate it though. The building doesn't have any windows. It's like being in a tomb all day."

"Some jobs are like that. Why don't you quit?"

"I can't afford to quit, and the economy around here is so bad that there aren't many opportunities for employment."

Larry remembered the sign at the Lost Bazaar. "I bet you're an artist of some kind."

She pulled back a little and looked at him. "I paint and sculpt. How did you know?"

"Lucky guess." He touched her left hand resting on his shoulder. "You have the hands of an artist, Delia."

"This is incredible. My friends know my love for art, but they never talk with me about it, never truly comment on my work when they see it. And then I meet you, and it's the first thing you say. Hey, I've got a reception tomorrow at an art gallery right around the corner called the Lost Bazaar. Maybe you can come and see my show."

"I'll check my busy schedule, but I ought to be able to make it."

The dance ended but Larry held on to her a moment and stared into her blue eyes.

"What is it?" she asked.

"You remind me of one of my daughters."

"Is that a good thing?"

"I don't know. She is the only one who will still talk to me. Her sisters and her mother, well—let's just say we don't communicate anymore."

"It's their loss, Larry. Their loss."

Larry drank and danced with Delia until the band counted down the last few seconds of the year. When the clock struck midnight, the crowd shouted "Happy New Year!" and tooted plastic trumpets and a few couples kissed. When the band launched into a blue grass version of "Auld Lang Syne," Larry's mind wandered back—to last year, the year before, and the year before that. This was the first New Year's Eve he hadn't been with them. He wondered what his daughters were doing tonight.

"Who is old man Zyne?" Delia asked.

"He's the good times long ago in our past. The song originally had several verses. I'll quote them if you want."

"Let's save that for another time." Delia leaned forward and kissed him on the lips. "Happy New Year, Larry," she said.

He placed his hand on her cheek. "Happy New Year, Delia. May it be your best."

Delia blushed, then cleared her throat. "I need to leave now, Larry. See you tomorrow?"

"Sure." Larry watched her leave, waiting for her to turn back and look at him one more time. She didn't. "I'm sorry your friends didn't come, Delia," he whispered.

At 1:00 AM the bar manager shouted, "Folks, you don't have to go home, but you can't stay here."

Larry returned to his chair scooping up an unfinished whiskey as the crowd filed out—some left alone, others were headed for trysting places or after-hours clubs. "No thanks, folks. I think I'll just stick around here," he said to no one in particular.

On his way out, he stuffed his pockets with leftover peanuts and pretzels. Picking up another half-finished drink, he downed it quickly, and the straight whiskey warmed his throat and belly. He set down the glass and looked around for Preacher, but he couldn't find him. Trying not to think of the damp cold he knew would seep into his bones before morning, he walked out of the bar into the darkness of the gravel parking lot.

The rain had ended. Larry sat with his back against the floodwall where he could see the river. He was relieved he hadn't gotten drunk tonight and passed out in the bar. A man ought to choose his resting-place. It's bad when the drink decides. Too many things are lost that way. He fastened the Velcro collar of his jacket and pulled his cap lower. There was no breeze, and the thick moist air was heavy and full of the sour rotten smell of the paper mill. The stillness oppressed him and pushed his thoughts and being into his own flesh.

Weariness crept up his legs and he closed his eyes and drifted into sleep. His mind was empty at first, but his dreams carried him into the Lost Bazaar where he saw himself and others he did not know hanging on its walls. Barkers and auctioneers in fancy suits stood in front of the gallery hustling indifferent people on the busy street to come in and buy the people on display in honor of the good times past. Larry hung near the door above the statue of the tormented man. One of the auctioneers cursed and flogged him with a whip while Larry raised his fists and howled in pain. Delia passed by and he cried out to her for help. Someone gouged his ribs with a metal rod.

"Hey you! Wake up."

Larry looked up through his blurred eyes into the face of a policeman. "Oh. Mornin', officer."

"What are you doing here?" He tapped his open hand with his nightstick.

"Sleeping," Larry said.

"Don't you have somewhere to stay? Did you get drunk and pass out here?"

"It's a long story. Do you really want to know?"

"Can I see some identification, sir?"

"Don't have any. Don't need it anymore."

"Look, smart ass, before I get real curious about who you are, you better get up and move on or I'll carry your indigent ass to jail. You can't stay here."

"I've heard that before. I'm going."

Larry rose and plodded back to the Lost Bazaar. Preacher sat on the curb.

"I thought you might be coming back this way," Preacher said.

"Where did you sleep?" Larry asked.

"In the back of a truck at the bar, but this mornin' a feller woke me up and the truck was at some apartments. He seemed pretty riled up. Where'd you sleep?"

"Down by the river. They're having a reception here this morning. We can get some coffee and breakfast if we hang around a while."

"That's a fine idea, King Larry. Mighty fine."

A huge cloud of blackbirds flew over them, filling the air with the sound of their wings and chirping. Splotches of white splattered the ground around them, and Larry felt a gob of bird shit hit his jacket.

Preacher snickered. "Louisiana's got lots of those blackbirds, don't it? They're like people—you gotta watch out for them when they're in big groups."

They waited on the curb. The gallery had just opened when Delia arrived. She stepped out of the BMW wearing a black formal dress. A man in a suit accompanied her.

Preacher slapped Larry on the shoulder. "She's come to see you, Larry! And all dolled up too. Wonder who the man in that fancy suit is. He must not know you two have a thing going on."

"She didn't come to see me. She's the featured artist you dumb ass. I don't know who the guy is. And be careful what you say. They might be married or something. Delia and I don't have a thing going on anyway."

They followed the crowd into the gallery and Preacher sped directly to a table loaded with refreshments. Larry strolled through the gallery and studied Delia's paintings and sculptures, pausing at the bronze man-statue he had seen through the window yesterday. Delia noticed Larry and wended her way through the crowd to him.

"Larry!" she said. "You did make it."

"I want to congratulate the featured artist. Your art is exceptional, Delia."

"Thanks, Larry."

Larry nodded toward the man in the suit. "Your husband?"

"It's a long story, Larry."

"It's okay. We're all long stories in one way or another. Have you sold anything?"

"A few paintings," she said.

"If I had the money, I'd buy this creature-man-next-to-the-sad-woman-statue to remember you by."

"That's sweet of you to say, Larry." She touched the statue's eyes. "It's my favorite piece. I call it, *Tempest in the Mind*."

The man in the suit walked over and took Delia by the arm. "I don't mean to interrupt your conversation with this—gentleman, Delia, but I think one of my friends wants to buy a painting." He glanced at Larry and smirked.

Delia sighed and Larry thought he saw a flash of anger in her eyes. "Excuse me, Larry. Enjoy yourself. Maybe we can talk more later." She placed her hand on Larry's arm and squeezed. "Take care of yourself, Larry."

Preacher walked over as Larry was studying the man-statue. Preacher bent over and peered at it closely. "Lord! He ain't got no eyeballs!"

"I'd buy this statue if I had the money, Preacher."

"What do you want a graven image for, King Larry?" he shouted. "You can't afford nothing like this. Besides, he don't seem like he'd be good for anything."

"You're right, Preacher. See you later." Larry scooped up the statue and ran out of the gallery toward the Cottonport Lounge.

Preacher hollered, "Hey, Larry! Ain't you gonna eat first?" He grabbed a platter of pastries from the table and ran after him. "Hold on, King Larry, I'm right behind you!"

Several in the crowd pursued them. The man with Delia strode to the gallery's desk and picked up the phone. "Delia, I had a bad feeling about that man from the moment I first saw him. I'll call the police."

Delia took the receiver from his hand and set it on the hook. "No. No police."

"Are you crazy? You can't let that homeless bum steal your art!"

"It's mine to let go. Leave him alone. At least *he* liked it."

When Larry reached the floodwall, he turned and saw the crowd in pursuit.

Preacher yelled, "You sure do know how to raise Cain. Shall we gather at the river, King Larry?"

Larry willed his rubbery legs toward the river and jumped into the cold water. Preacher stopped at the edge and stuffed a pastry into his mouth. "You done lost your mind, King Larry. This ain't no time to go baptizing yourself. Get out and eat one of these cinnamon rolls."

Larry crooked his arm around the neck of the statue and sidestroked into deep water as if he were a lifeguard rescuing a drowning man. The river carried him downstream past the houseboats, past the plush houses and apartments built along the riverbank. Larry struggled to cut across the Ouachita so he could reach the Monroe side, but the current denied him any progress and sapped his strength. Vice-like invisible hands pulled at him, and a Lethean numbness crept up his legs. Through blurred eyes Larry glanced at the bronze face in the crook of his arm.

"Damn, you're a heavy one, but I ain't gonna let you go. You don't belong in no Lost Bazaar. How long you reckon a man can hold his breath?"

Larry raised a fist to the sky and howled at the crowd on the riverbank, then let the river pull them down.

# A Very Small Splash

About suffering they were never wrong, / The Old Masters: how well they understood / Its human position—"Muée des Beaux Arts"
by W. H. Auden.

No one answers the door, so I walk around to the back porch where I thought I'd find her. She's barefoot on the wood decking, wearing cut-off jeans and a white tank top. The wind plays with her long straight strawberry-blonde hair, stroking and teasing it out with invisible delicate fingers.

"Hey, Shelby," I say.

She nods, but does not speak. She chews thoughtfully on the end of her paintbrush, then studies her painting, which I knew to be her fourth attempted interpretation of Brueghel's *The Fall of Icarus*. On the canvas, I recognize the aqua-blue water of Acapulco Bay, and the white legs of her Icarus protruding from the water, vainly kicking the air. A piss-poor Mexican peasant, oblivious to the drowning Icarus, plows behind a burro. His face favors mine. An American Airlines plane trails vapors across the sky. I notice that Shelby left herself out of the painting this time.

\*\*\*

Travis, my best friend, worked for A.G. Edwards. He always listened carefully when his clients talked to him about Acapulco. What he heard in their stories, and what he saw in their pictures infected him. He saw Acapulco as a magical city, full of romance and good times, a lush island of prosperity surrounded by beautiful mountains, a city glutted with the money of glitterati and jetsetters. Travis decided he had to go there, and that I should go too.

"Shelby and I are going to Acapulco, and we want you to go with us. You need to take a break from school, man. I'm making money hand over fist, so I'll even pay for your ticket. Besides, you speak Spanish. What do you say? Couldn't you use an unforgettable vacation?"

31

"Sure," I said. "Most of my vacations have been quite forgettable. Just ask me. But wouldn't you rather take the trip by yourselves?"

"Shelby won't mind. She thinks a lot of you, man. Besides, you're my best friend. I can't take a trip like this without you. I'll take care of everything."

What was sad about this conversation was that I probably really was his best friend. Travis talked like I had never dated Shelby. Like the suave Don Juan he is hadn't swept her off her feet and taken her out of my life. Like if it had been anyone but him, I probably would have throttled him. One of us was in serious delusion or denial.

"Okay. I couldn't take off very long," I said. "I've got comps coming up."

He slapped my shoulder. "The studies. Always your studies. A few days off will do you good. Leave the arrangements to me."

Two weeks later, the three of us boarded an American Airlines jet and left for Acapulco.

***

Señor Frog's was not far from our hotel, so we walked to the club via the beach. We entered, paid the twenty-dollar door, and moved to the bar.

The club was packed out with tourists and upper class Mexicans. Our senses were assaulted by the sights and sounds swirling about us. High-energy techno music dug into our guts and the strobe lights froze the ecstatic dancers into shifting, frozen tableaus.

"Things are hopping at Señor Frog's tonight, aren't they, Sheridan?" Travis said. "God, I love this place already—wild, exotic, money everywhere. I need to learn Spanish, Sheridan. Maybe some of that laundered drug money can come my way. It's going to be invested somewhere. Might as well be with me. I thought about paying Miguel to teach me."

"Shit, Travis. Learning Spanish from your Tex-Mex janitor would be like learning English from a redneck."

"Well, I'm glad you're with us. Ask that waiter to get us a table with a view."

"Two to one, everyone working here speaks English, Travis. Since they make so much money from tourists, they have to be pretty good with it."

I signaled a waiter and gave him our request. A couple of drinks later, he moved us to a table. Through the tinted glass walls I looked out on Acapulco Bay, dotted with the lights of fishing boats and ocean liners. Two guitarists and a singer in sombreros came up to our table. They wore bandoleers filled with shot glasses. They sang us a short ballad about the Rey Sol tequila they were advertising and gave us each a filled shot glass. Travis asked to buy a bottle, and the singer went to fetch it. He shelled out the $350.00 and gave the girl who brought the bottle a twenty-dollar tip.

The trio moved on to the next table. One of the four Mexican girls resisted drinking her shot. Her friends held open her mouth while the singer poured the tequila down her throat. Her friends laughed, clapped, and cheered the choking girl, and the pleased troubadours moved on.

A club worker came by and took a Polaroid picture of us for their bulletin board. She offered to take another, which she would give to us for five dollars. I paid her, and we posed again, our arms around each other, Shelby sitting between Travis and me. We saluted the camera with our shot glasses.

Travis slid the bottle of tequila toward me. "Enjoy, Sheridan. Shelby and I are going to dance."

I watched them dance—Shelby restrained, but smiling, Travis, performing a wild tarantella. When I couldn't stand any more of that sight, I studied the face on the round bottle of Rey Sol Anejo designed for the company by Sergio Bustamante, an artist from Guadalajara. I remembered seeing a bronze sculpture of his in a Brownsville art gallery—*Sol en Enamorado.*

I could see a trace of my own reflection mingling with the sun-face on the bottle's front. I couldn't tell if the face was grimacing or smiling. "You have a sad face," I said to the bottle.

Shelby and Travis returned, and we slammed down Coronas and Rey Sol until my head spun. I placed my hand over my shot glass when Travis tried to fill it with more.

"What's wrong, Sheridan? Drink up! Don't wimp out on me." Travis stood on his chair and gyrated to the beat of the music. He held out his arms as if they were wings. "Look, Sheridan! I'm flying! Let's see how high we can get."

"Don't get mad-dog crazy on us, Travis. You're going to get us thrown out—even if this is Mexico."

"Wimp."

"I'm not a wimp. I just need to pace myself. You do too."

"Travis," Shelby said. "I've had enough. If I drink any more, I'll be sick. I want to go back to our room."

"Well, hell. Go."

"I don't think I can walk straight, and I'm scared to go by myself."

"Sheridan will walk you to the room. Won't you, buddy?"

"Yeah, and then I'll come back and drag your drunk ass back too."

"I can always count on you, Sheridan," Travis said.

Shelby wobbled when she stood up. She put her arm around my neck, and whispered, "Thank you, Sheridan."

With her arm around my waist, she managed the walk down the beach, but I had to sling her over my shoulder in a fireman's carry to get her up the stairs. Once in her room, she kicked off her sandals and fell on the bed. I held her hand as she fell asleep.

I brushed her hair from her eyes and whispered, "We never got to spend a whole night together."

Then, I went back for Travis.

\*\*\*

Travis had left our table to join the four Mexican girls next to us. He was still slamming down Coronas and tequila. When he saw me, he said, "Sheridan! Amigo! Come and join us. I've some new friends I want you to meet. This is Veronica, Maria, Carmen, and Felina. They don't speak English very well, so help me out here."

"*Hola, señoritas.*" All four were beautiful. I sat down between Veronica and Felina. Felina smiled. I looked her in the eye and said, "*Sus ojos son como las estrellas del cielo.*"

"*Gracias,*" she said. She covered her face with her hand and giggled. Her friends laughed and began teasing her. "Felina *tiene un novio quapo!*"

"What am I missing here, Sheridan?" Travis said. "They're talking about me, right?"

"Right," I said. Travis continued to spiral into his wildness, especially flirting with Felina, and I talked with Veronica. She told me they were from Guadalajara and that they had saved for three years to be able to take this trip. Travis and I danced with each of the girls in turn. While slow dancing with Veronica, I discovered she could speak a little English. She said, "Felina likes your friend very much. But I don't think this good. Travis has *novia*? The girl who was here before?"

"Wife. But it's not my business." I looked up just as Travis and Felina kissed. It made me think of the first time I saw him kiss Shelby, a little over a year ago.

"But he is your friend?"

"Yeah. My friend."

When the girls went to the restroom, Travis placed another shot and Corona in front of me. My blurred eyes saw two beer bottles instead of one.

"Sheridan," he said. "Felina is making me crazy. She looked at me with those black pearl eyes, and I melted. But they sparkle—almost like they've caught the sun. I think I'm in love."

"Nothing about you is original, Travis. You took that line from one of my short stories. You're in love, but with Shelby. You've had too much tequila. What are you doing? You've got a good woman. You ought to appreciate her."

"Felina wants me to come to her room when we leave."

"Did somebody sell you some mushrooms?"

"And get this. Felina has to go back to Guadalajara early tomorrow. They were going to take the bus back, but I offered to rent a car and drive them down. I'll take a plane or bus back day after tomorrow. Shelby's so drunk she'll be hung over all day. Tell her I had an emergency call—some A.G. Edwards contacts there or something and I'll be back late, day after tomorrow."

"Look, you don't want to go to Guadalajara," I said. "My father was right: Mexico makes people crazy." My father had grown up along the border. At my age, he had done the wild-in-Mexico thing, but something had happened in Matamores that made him hate Mexico and vow never to return. He said there was something there that put too much darkness and foolishness in people's heads.

"Well, if you go, please fly back." Somehow I didn't think Travis would enjoy a long Mexican bus ride.

"You want to go?" he asked.

"Hell, no. And you shouldn't either. You'll be a white Anglo in a sea of brown faces. You don't speak Spanish, and you'll need that in Guadalajara. But even if you did speak Spanish well, somebody there might think you were DEA and shoot your ass. Another thing, this girl seems to come from a conservative family. This isn't the states. Mexican fathers can be very protective."

"Oh, come on. What he could he do?"

"Plenty. He could pay a local policeman twenty bucks to plant some drugs on you. He could pay someone thirty dollars to shoot you and bury you in a shallow ditch. Just on his word, he could have you arrested for rape. Do you know what Mexican prisons are like? A white man would have to fight every day of shitty and probably very short life. Christ, you don't know shit about Mexico."

Felina and her friends made their way back to our table. They didn't look as beautiful as they had moments before.

"Never mind, Sheridan," Travis said. "I think you're full of shit. Just tell Shelby what I said, and try to cover my ass." He handed me a credit card. "Take her shopping. Spend some money. Now, let's get done to some serious drinking."

***

*Señor. Señor.*

I raised my face from the forest of beer bottles on the table and peered through my tequila beaten eyes into the face of a waiter.

"I am sorry to wake you, *Señor*, but the bus boys need to clean the table."

"What time is it?"

He patted me on the back. "Seven in the morning, *Señor*. You have good time in Acapulco?"

"*Sí. Como no.* Where's my friend?"

"*¿Mande?*"

"*Mi amigo. ¿Donde Esta?*"

"I do not know your friend, *Señor*."

I stood up on my rubbery legs, and my stomach rolled. It was not going to be a good day. Shelby wouldn't be the only one with a hangover. The club workers continued their cleanup without looking at me. I was grateful for their politeness. I returned to my room and fell asleep.

Late that afternoon, Shelby pounded on my door till I answered.

"Time to wake up, sleepy head," she said. "I got tired of sitting around my room. God, you look awful." Her face was cheerful, beaming, and she was as beautiful as ever. Evidently, Travis had projected his own drunken condition onto her. A plastic sack hung on her arm.

"Where's Travis?" she asked.

"I don't know."

"You don't have any idea where he is?"

"Shit, Shelby. I passed out at the club. Woke up face down this morning on a table. But he did say something about going to Guadalajara today to wrap some A. G. Edwards business."

"With who?"

"Travis was never one to tell me what he really had on his mind when he's up to something." Her face didn't reveal she understood my real meaning. "He said he'd be back day after tomorrow." I remembered the credit card in my wallet. "He gave me his credit card and said for us to go shopping and spent some money."

"Well, get dressed and let's go." She looked me up and down, but not like she used to. "Though you are cute in those boxers." She opened up the sack and held up a very small thong bikini. "Let's go to the beach too. How do you like my new suit?"

"It will look great on you." I really wished she hadn't done that.

\*\*\*

37

Two days later, Travis still hadn't returned and wouldn't answer his cell. We were due to be out of our rooms in four days. Shelby and I had seen every tourist site, drank ourselves senseless both nights, and were too sunburned to spend any more time on the beach. I'm not going to say I didn't have fun, because I did. Life with Shelby without Travis. When she and I had dated, we were both in college working on our degrees and had little time for and money to do anything like this. On the other hand, we were both worried about Travis. Travis had always counted on his charisma, and his ability to wing his way out of difficult situations. But I knew those tactics didn't always work in Mexico. There's too many variables here.

Early the third morning, Shelby came to my room and sat silently on the edge of my bed. She was inward and obviously depressed.

"Okay," I said. "If he doesn't call tonight, I'll get on the hotel phone and try to run him down. If I have to, I'll go to Guadalajara and try to find his sorry ass."

"Thanks, Sheridan." She said it sincerely, but she didn't smile, then she leaned over and kissed me on the cheek.

I wished she hadn't done that.

***

Travis finally called, explaining that the business had been more promising then expected. He told Shelby he wanted me to come down to see him. I used his credit card and took a small plane to the airport, then a cab to the hotel. I found him in the hotel restaurant, eating flour tortillas and fried eggs. He smiled and waved me over to his table.

"Sheridan! Want some breakfast, buddy?"

"Coffee will do. You ass hole. Shelby's worried sick about you."

"I'm really working, Sheridan. Some good opportunities came my way here."

"Yeah, sure."

"I really have. Four new accounts. These are big ones, too. And I've made arrangements with corporate to open a branch of our Dallas office here, so it looks like I'll be coming back to this fine city a good bit. And you were worried about me."

"What happened with Felina?"

"Oh, she's up in the room. Likes to look really pretty for breakfast. Sure you don't want anything?"

"Yeah, I'm sure."

"I even met her family. Lied about being married of course. The father got real excited when I offered to invest in the family business. I think it's some sort of export store—chimeneas, pottery, rugs, those sorts of things."

"Well, besides you becoming a sorry bastard, what's the story? I've got to go back to Dallas."

"You two go on back. I'll fly up next week. Listen, don't say anything specific about this to Shelby, but to be honest, I don't know if Shelby and I are going to work out. This girl has really fucked up my head. I'm in love like I've never been, Sheridan. I know I've got to call Shelby and tell her something. I'll do that tonight."

"Sure." I drained my coffee. "But don't call and tell her. At least have the decency to come back to Acapulco and see us off. Our flight is the day after tomorrow. Be there. See you later." I left the table without looking at him.

***

I hailed a cab at the Acapulco airport. The driver chattered constantly talking to me over the Tejano and Mariachi music blaring from his radio.

I waved a fifty-dollar bill. "Do you know this town well?"

He looked in his rearview mirror and saw the bill. "Yes, very well. How can I be of assistance?"

"I need a favor. A very personal favor."

His eyes were glued on the face of General Grant. "I am sure I can help you, whatever your *need* may be."

I handed him the fifty. "I need a name of a policeman who can be trusted. One who would help me with a personal problem I have. Of course, I'd be happy to pay him well."

"What is the nature of your problem?"

"An American I know is trying to take advantage of a Mexican girl. She is the very young daughter of a prominent Guadalajara businessman."

39

"This is very serious. You are the girl's *novio*?"

"No, just a friend of the family. So, do you know a policeman who can help me? This American I'm speaking of is very sly."

"I will take you to one now. He is a very good friend."

"*Gracias.*"

We drove to an intersection where an officer was directing traffic. The drive pointed to him. "There's my friend. I think he would be delighted to help you. He himself had a daughter that ran off with a *gringo*. His shame and pain was very great."

"He will be fine. Would you talk to him and see if he's interested?"

He parked the cab and walked to the policeman. They left the intersection and the motorist from all four directions were left to navigate as best they could. A moment later, the policeman walked over to me. He was all smiles.

"I am Captain Hernandez, and I understand you have a problem. I can be of assistance, but such police work requires you pay me for my time."

"A hundred American dollars," I said.

He nods. "This is acceptable. I assume you look for a permanent solution to your problem."

"Yes." I was amazed how money made everything so simple in Mexico.

He handed me a small notebook. "I need his name and where I can find him." As I was writing, he looked at Acapulco Bay, bathed in sunlight, full of ocean liners, yachts and fishing boats. Sun worshippers speckled the beach, and hang gliders soared and dipped through the sky. An American Airlines jet roared overhead, a white trail marking its route. "So many tourists come here to find themselves, but Acapulco can also be very treacherous, so they find what they do not expect. Terrible accident can happen. Some try to fish or swim the bay under the influence of drugs. They sometimes fall off their boats. I have found few men who can make it back to shore in such a condition. One gringo tried to imitate the divers from the cliffs, not realizing how much skill is required."

"When one flies too high, the crash is great," I said as I handed him his notebook and the hundred-dollar bill.

Sheridan's body was found in the bay near the beach two days later. The autopsy indicated he was full of drugs and that somehow his legs and arms had been broken.

\*\*\*

Shelby lashes out at the painting with her brush, mutilating her day's work. She kicks the easel over, sits down on the deck and sobs.

I watch the painting fall from the porch and sail to the ground. On the smeared canvass, I can barely see the pair of white legs protruding from the aqua-blue bay, and in my head I hear a very small splash.

# Apollo Descends

I remember all the ruckus about that movie they called *The Fight Club*. Shoot. I live on a farm outside of Hendrix, Oklahoma, where we been having barn fights rougher than that since Indian Territory days. Fights where the blood is real, and the bruises deep, and where a man can make one careless move and be stove up for a month.

My daddy said the old Chickasaw masters had some white man vices in them and enjoyed watching their slaves duke it out with slaves from other plantations and ranches. Well, after General Stand Watie surrendered to the Federals in 1865, slavery ended in Indian Territory, but the barn fights didn't stop. No, sir. The rich Chickasaws switched to gamblin' on their sharecropper and field hand fighters. They knew a poor man will do about anything for a chance to climb out of his misfortune. They'd throw a little money to the winners so they could feel better about using them so, but the fighters didn't mean nothin' to them. Barnfights were their recreation. They didn't lose a bit of sleep over broken jaws, busted hands, or bruised ribs. The rich farmers called the fighters *Southern Gladiators* and talked with admiration of how these men were fightin' for a better life, but I think they just wanted to get the poor man's hopes up with such talk and keep the gristmill turning so more fighters would come their way. I've watched many a man step in this gristmill, saw many a man make some money and win a woman's eye, but I never saw one that could fight himself enough to get out of the fightin' once he got the big head and started winning.

I know about the barn fights because my son Phorbas was a barn fighter for a long time. No one could whip him till ole Sol came along.

That was a long time ago. I'm an old man now, but I still come to the fights. I can spot the old hands. The moment a fighter steps up to the scratch line and peels off his shirt and I see his scars and the way he carries himself, I can tell how tired, how drunk, and how scared he is. Most new fighters are rattled, unsettled by the blood and ruthlessness of it all. There's a new fighter tonight, a big white boy, and I can tell he ain't scared at all. When the boy's face turned, I saw how his eyes were the same as a wild-eyed dog that you knew was bout to bite you. He's one of the mean ones who are always fightin' with something, even if it's just himself. He weren't drinkin' like the others, just leaning against the post, arms crossed, with almost a bored look on his face. Just like Phorbas used to do. I reached in my overalls pocket for a wad of bills, thumbed through them, and decided to bet on him tonight. Directly, he looked me right in the eye, half-smiled, and nodded his head. Yes, sir, he and I knew this would be his night.

Mr. Rainwater sponsors the barn fights now, just like Mr. Colbert used to do when Phorbas was on this earth. I saw him across the room collecting money, and I walked over to him.

"How you doin', Jacob?" he said.

"I's fine Mr. Rainwater, I's fine."

"You bettin' tonight?" he asked.

"Yessuh, I'm goin' to bet on that white boy yonder. Who is he?" I handed him fifty dollars.

"Some boy from West Texas. And he's an arrogant son of a bitch. You're the only one bettin' on him so far. If you win, you'll win big."

"He reminds me of Phorbas years ago."

"That's what I just said."

I looked at him. "Phorbas weren't always that way, Mr. Rainwater. I made him that way, getting him started in these barn fights."

"Phorbas was a man who made his own choices, Jacob. We got to let them grow up on their own, even if they do make a mess of it. He was a good fighter—none better, till ole Sol rose up. He's in the pen now."

"Who's in the pen?"

"Ole Sol. The law sent him down to Huntsville after he killed a man in a barn fight in Athens, Texas."

"Don't bother me none that he's in the pen. He should have gone to the pen for what he done to Phorbas." I opened my pocketknife and cut a sliver from the Bull of the Woods tobacco plug and slipped it into my mouth.

"That was a most unfortunate night, Jacob," Mr. Rainwater said. "Yeah, Phorbas was a good fighter, till all his winning went to his head. He messed up when he started drinkin' and livin' hard like all these others here. Started thinkin' no one could beat him. But there's always someone who can whip you. Always is."

"Yes, suh. Always is."

Phorbas believed anybody could be whipped—anybody but him, but I should've told Phorbas that he was wrong, that there ain't no mortal man who can't be whipped somehow. I guess deep down, I didn't want to believe no one could whip him, and he was making so much money that I sure didn't want to discourage him none. That was over twenty years ago, when Phorbas had his first fight, but I remembered it well.

\*\*\*

PHORBAS and me were plowing a new acre of land I'd won from my bets the last winter. One morning after our breakfast of leftover fried cornmeal mush and sorghum syrup, we walked down to the field. I put Phorbas to plowing while I snaked logs out of the field with our other mule. Phorbas righted the plow and got right to work. He weren't no lazy boy.

"Come on, jenny," he said. He snapped the reins and the mule moved forward, and the iron blade he had filed the night before bit into the black bottomland dirt. Directly, the plowshare hung up on a stump root. "Hold, jenny," Phorbas said. He lifted the plow handle, and I could see the blade was bent nearly straight back. After he laid the plow on its side, he pounded the blade with his grapefruit-sized fist until the metal bent back to its original shape. He righted the plow, jackhammered the point into the ground, and said, "Go on, mule," and then went right back to work.

"Lord, have mercy," I said. "Phorbas!"

Phorbas reined the mule to a stop and turned toward me. "Yessir?"

"Stop working and get you a drank."

He walked over, and I handed him a dipper of water. I studied him a minute, picturing that big fist of his connecting to someone's head and making us a passel of money. Phorbas was a big boy—nearly six-foot tall, with muscles like I never had. He could lift a 500 pound cotton bale by himself and pitch hay bales for ten hours on the hottest of days.

I let him take a good drink, and then I said, "I'm mite proud of you, Phorbas, graduatin' from high school and all. You learn anything from all those fights you's always getting in at school?"

"I learnt it's best to not get hit yourself."

"You never lost a fight, did you?"

"Not even close, daddy. Most of them I only had to hit once and they went down. Ain't nobody round here to fight no more."

"A man can always find someone to fight. What if I was to enter you in a little boxin' match so we could make a little money? Let you use up some of that extra nervous energy you got."

"I don't know. How much money you talking about?"

"How much you making workin' for me?"

"I ain't makin nothin' workin' for you."

"Be a whole lot more than that."

Phorbas grinned. "Shore. Making some money would be good for a change."

"You finish up the field. I got some business in town," I said. "You get cleaned up a little. We might go back later."

"Yessir," Phorbas said. "I ain't been to town in a long time. And you ain't never took me in on a Saturday night." Phorbas wiped his bare chest with the rag he had looped on the plow-pole.

"Well, after tonight, you'll know where I been going." I took my mule to the barn, and walked down what we call Peanut Trail toward Kemp. When I reached Mr. Colbert's store, I stepped inside and pulled an orange pop out of the icebox. I laid down a quarter for the pop. "Mr. Colbert, I want to talk to you about the fight tonight."

"Sure. You wanting to bet?"

"Yessir, I got me a little money I can put down. I want to bet on a new fighter."

"Who's that, Jacob? Who? Big John from Stillwater is the only new fighter I heared of."

"No, suh. I want to enter my boy Phorbas into this here contest. You reckon he can make some money at one of these fights?"

"If he wins, he can walk out with a pocketful. But pshaw, Jacob. Phorbas, big and strong as he is, ain't no barn-fighter. He ain't ever been in a fight like this before. Barn fightin's not at all like a schoolyard fight. Odds won't be in his favor."

"Phorbas ain't a schoolboy no more. I learnt that today. He's ready." I laid down fifty dollars. "I want to bet this on him. Phorbas is gonna win tonight." I pushed the stack of bills toward Colbert.

Colbert picked up the money, then shook his head. "You ain't got enough money to be throwing it away like this, Jacob."

"I earned every cent of this money, and it's mine to throw away if I'm a mind to."

"Alright. But I think this is about a hair-brained scheme as you ever come up with. And Phorbas is the one who'll hurt over it."

"We'll see you tonight," I said.

Phorbas and I ate a supper of cornbread, turnip greens, and purple-hull peas, then walked down the highway together. We had walked about a mile when I said, "Folks say there's a black boy from Stillwater who calls hisself Big John. He be comin' to the barn fights and bragging he cain't be beaten. This afternoon I bet some money that you could whip him. This here's a chance for you to make some good money. Those hands of yours are a gift from the Lord. You think you can handle this boy?"

"I ain't found no man yet I couldn't whip."

We cut up the dirt road off the Kemp Highway that led up to Hebert's farm. We walked behind his house to the barn where the fighters and the gamblers had gathered.

Mr. Colbert was there, and he held a clipboard on which he had the fighters matched. When he saw us, he said, "Phorbas. You and Big John are the two newest fighters. You go first. Let's see what you got, boy."

While the men in the barn were cheering and placing last minute bets, Big John slowly circled Phorbas. Big John's hands moved continuously in a circular motion in front of him. Phorbas' elbows were pressed against his body, the fists close, protective of his face. At first, Phorbas circled with him, but then he set himself, dropped his hands, and didn't move at all,. When Big John moved in, Phorbas' front hand snapped out and that big fist of his flattened that Stillwater boy.

The crowd got real quiet, looking at Big John lying there on the floor, like they couldn't hardly believe the fight was already over.

Mr. Colbert nudged big John with his boot, then held up Phorbas' arm. "Here's the winner. Pay up gentlemen." He pointed at me. "Give this boy's money to his daddy there. Let's get Big John out of here."

"What's they going to do with Big John?" Phorbas asked.

"They'll put him out along the road somewhere," I said.

"What if'n he needs a doctor?" Phorbas said.

"He can get to one tomorrow, I reckon. Ain't our concern, Phorbas. That's the way it is in the barn fights."

"What if'n a man was to die?"

"Then they'd leave him in front of a funeral home. They got undertakers at the fights now and then. They be glad to get the business."

"A hurt or dead man shouldn't be done like that, just throwed out like he weren't no good."

"Ain't no good way for a man to die, Phorbas," I said. "But don't you worry about it none. There ain't no one in the county that can whip you."

Then I'll be durned if Mr. Colbert didn't do something strange. He pulled me aside and said, " Tell Phorbas not to knockout a man so quick. Drag it out next time, play the crowd. Know who's betting on him. He'll make more money. Some of the men like to watch a spell before they bet."

Phorbas didn't pal around with many, but he did have one white friend that he favored. Called himself Brandon. He was a strange sort of bird with wild hair like that Mr. Don King I saw once on Mr. Colbert's television. Neither Brandon nor Phorbas had a regular job. Phorbas said there weren't no need to wear himself out with shift-work at the Pillsbury plant when he could make enough money in one night of fighting to buy all the whiskey and women he wanted for a month. I wanted to make life easier for Phorbas when I got him into this fightin', but looking back, I don't think he was suited for it. Phorbas turned mean and kept getting into scraps with people in town who didn't know about his fighting abilities. That temper and mouth of his got him put in the Bryan County caboose a few times and he was fined pretty heavy. Eventually, Phorbas got so wild I could hardly recognize my own boy. He got a notion to look like someone he called Jimmy Hendrix, so he let his hair bush out like Brandon's. He said that once he retired from fighting, he wanted to learn to play guitar soon as he found someone who would teach him.

Brandon helped Phorbas get ready for the fights by giving him water and wrapping his hands. Phorbas was mighty particular about his hands, so he never would fight bare-knuckled. Brandon would wrap each of Phorbas's hands with some strips of soft leather, once around his knuckles, then a diagonal wrap across palm, then he would tape or tie it off. Brandon had told him that was how the ancient Greek fighters did it. Whilst they got ready, they talked about who Phorbas would fight that night. The last time I saw my boy fight, the night he fought ole Sol, I was sitting behind him and I heard them talking.

"I ain't looked at the roster. Who am I fighting tonight?" Phorbas asked Brandon.

Brandon tore off a piece of tape with his teeth and wrapped it around the leather on Phorbas's wrist. "You got one white boy," Brandon said. "He looks burned out and I don't think he will give you any trouble. He's got too big a belly to be a boxer. And his shins are too thick, so he won't be able to move round much. I think he'll go down quick. The other one's name is Sol. He's a black boy who's been winning fights over in Athens and Bonham. I'd shore watch him close. He's near as big as you, Phorbas. That's him over yonder."

Phorbas eyed the black man across the room. Sol had a woman in his lap and a bottle of beer in his hand. He locked eyes with Phorbas and hooted, "That's it! Give me some of that padding. I mean to retire you out good. Yes sir, this is probably your last barn fight. They'll find you in your car on the highway in the morning."

"Aw, Sol, I think he's kinda cute," the girl said.

"You hear that, meathead?" Sol said. "My no-good sister thinks you're cute. But my folks used to drop her on her head now and then, so I wouldn't pay Diane here no mind."

"That high yellar is an arrogant son of a bitch, ain't he, Phorbas?" Brandon said. "Why don't you just fight bare knuckle tonight? Ain't no reason to worry bout padding your blows on this man."

Phorbas pounded each fist twice into the palm of the opposite hand. "I ain't worried bout protecting his face. Just don't want to break my hand. If I break my hand, I can't fight no more and can't make no money." Phorbas coughed.

"You wheezing again?" Brandon said. "You better lay off those Kools."

"A few cigarettes ain't gonna kill me. A man's gotta have a few vices. I ain't lost a fight yet, have I?"

"No, and I don't reckon you oughta start tonight neither. But I know you're hungover, so you ain't gonna be at a hundred percent tonight, and this boy from Athens might be trouble. I was listenin' to some of the farmers. They's thinkin' your luck's going to run out."

"Aint no luck to winning a fight," Phorbas said as he stood and moved up to the scratch line. He and Sol eyed each other for a spell. Neither got in a real hurry, just circling each other, tapping out in the air, blowing once in a while like a deer that jumped out of a thicket.

Ole Sol sure knew how to box, almost like he had been the one to invent the sport. A natural—fast, strong, and vicious—just like Phorbas was. He knew things that Phorbas didn't. I lost a son and a bunch of money that night. After the fight, two of Mr. Hebert's friends helped me load Phorbas into my old Chrysler, and I drove him to Mr. Smith's funeral home up in Achille. Mr. Colbert offered to tote him up there for me, but since I was his daddy, I thought it was right for me to do it.

Yes, sir, that was a long time ago, but I ain't forgot that night yet. Much as I like coming to these barn fights, ever time I see a strong man go down, I think of my boy, and how Phorbas crumbled when Ole Sol laid into him. I saw him going down in my head again just as this new white boy flattened his third opponent for the night. The noise of the crowd softened inside my head, and it was no longer night. For a moment it was like I looked right into the sun. Then I could see the fields and the blue sky, and I was chasing a little Phorbas round the tree while his grandfather and the other field hands were picking strawberries. Then I saw an older Phorbas pitch one hay bale after another up on a flatbed truck. I was mighty proud of Phorbas. Before Phorbas went out on his own and before he started drinking so hard, he used to say that he couldn't have had a better daddy. I ain't made up my mind about that yet.

Good Lord! That West Texas boy's done knocked down another one . . . I reckon I'll go home with some money tonight.

# Adrift in Charleston

A man who finds the love of his life and then loses her is like a sailor adrift alone in the sea. If he ever does find himself back on solid ground, he is never quite the same.

Standing at the seawall along the Charleston Battery, I toasted Elizabeth with my Heineken and chugged down the last swallow. I heaved the bottle, as empty as myself, into the ocean. Like her, like us, the bottle vanished in the darkness in an instant. I suddenly felt old, rejected. I was 54, and I felt Elizabeth–my lover for a year, my best friend, my muse–had been my last chance–my last chance at finding the love of my life.

A late season Nor'easter had pounded the East Coast with rain and gale force winds and would soon hit Charleston. My flight out had been cancelled, and I was stuck alone in the city we should have traveled to together. I had sought refuge in a bar, but the jukebox had driven me outside, each song's story and each attached memory breaking my heart and making me think of her. Elizabeth was the woman in all those songs, just like she was the muse for the 300 poems I had written her the past year.

It's not easy to let her go.

Though only four in the afternoon, the dark clouds that always accompany a Nor'easter had blotted out the sun, and I could see nothing but the white foamy beards of waves crashing into the seawall.

The gusts of wind intensified. Soaked to the skin from the mist, I shivered. I listened to the wind, but unlike Elijah, I heard no still small voice to tell me what I should do. Elizabeth and I had once talked of Charleston, of coming here together. But our relationship had ended recently, not an angry, messy end–it had just ended. Not face to face, nor with a phone call, just with a few emails. Choices had been made, and I came up short. She said I had treated her like a queen the past year, and that I had been chivalrous, even in the way I accepted our "separation." I know I handled the break well on the outside, but inside I didn't do so well. A part of me wants her to be happy in the choice she made–but only a part. I know there's an ocean of women I could pursue, but I also know there's only one Elizabeth and that I could never love another like I love her.

A seagull lit on the seawall near me.

"Do you gulls really peck out a man's eyes when he's lost at sea?" I said. *Great,* I thought. *You're standing in the rain talking to seagulls. Shades of Poe.* The gull did a little dance, balancing herself on one leg, then the other, and like Poe's Raven, gave me no real answer to my question.

I heard a buoy ringing and saw its light in the darkness moving toward me, up the Ashley River. The heaving sobs of the ocean caused the four iron clappers inside its bronze bell to chant a dirge that matched my own mood. The storm must have severed the buoy's mooring, and like me, the buoy was doomed to be carried by some unseen current to some unknown destination. My gull flew off and lit on the buoy as if searching for a resting place before the coming storm. After a moment, she lifted her wings and the wind carried her into the dark sky and the buoy and I were left alone again.

A year ago, I had fallen in love with Elizabeth at first sight. Adrift in my own life and without map or lighthouse or compass to guide me, the past year I had held on to her like a drowning sailor clutching a spar. She was the only thing that had kept me afloat–she was my life buoy. Both of us were English teachers, and we taught our students literature's themes of love, loss, and longing. The hurricane we brewed in our year's romance taught us more about those timeless topics, and our breakup tutored me about the ephemeral nature of love. I imagined her in Mobile, Alabama with her ex this weekend. Good weather there according to the Weather Channel. I wondered what they might be doing. She would likely be in happy sunshine days and wouldn't imagine a lonely sailor (English teacher) standing in a storm, lost in the sea of love, fighting for his life and sanity, fighting the ocean's currents and the undertow that threatened to drag him to the bottom.

I closed my eyes, imagining Elizabeth standing with me now. I could see her in my mind, with her long strawberry blonde hair, her emerald green eyes, her freckled face, and her hand upon my arm. I suddenly found it hard to breathe. The sharp shards of her memory woke me from my reverie, and tired of the misting rain, I decided to return to the bar I had left earlier and face the music.

As I turned to leave the seawall, a flock of seagulls passed above my head and lit on a group of new buoys that had drifted into the bay. I heard gull cries mingle with the bells of the buoys, and they seemed indifferent to the fact that currents and wind would soon separate them. Maybe the gulls will return to the same buoys someday. Maybe Elizabeth will return to me. "Who knows what the future holds?" she had said in her last email. I studied the bobbing buoys, the gulls on top of them and thought that neither gulls nor buoys would be together there long. The storm was coming, and the buoys would soon be adrift, alone–just like me.

# Days of the Dead

Tell me how you die and I'll tell you who you are.—Octavio Paz
October 1999

Outside the Huntsville State Penitentiary, I waited for the bus. Glancing at the razor wire fence, I wondered what I had lost inside. Four years ago a drunk at a Halloween party decided he wanted to fight. I won the scrap, but nearly killed the man in the process, so Texas charged me with vicious assault and sent me to Huntsville, which in turn viciously assaulted me. I shook my head, willing the nightmares to vanish, but they clung—web-like, dirty.

Two other released inmates stood with me—Vic, a Mexican who had befriended me early in my sentence and another Mexican I didn't know. When the bus arrived, the stranger hurried toward the open door, bumping me.

"*Lo siento,*" he said.

"You just naturally clumsy, bean-eater, or do you work at it?" I said.

He wagged his finger. "Ah, the crazy one. Always angry and starting fights he can not win."

Vic stepped between us and placed his hand on my shoulder. "He is right, Justin. No trouble today, okay? We all leave Huntsville and go home." He patted me on the shoulder and nudged me toward the bus.

I gritted my teeth and stepped inside, sharing a seat with Vic. He grinned. "Is good to not be prisoner now, eh, Justin? But you do not seem happy."

"It doesn't seem real yet. My head's still inside."

He shifted his eyes toward the prison. "Who is to say when freedom is real? What will you do in Dallas?"

"I'm going to stay with my parents for a while. Let my head clear, find a job if I can. All that shit."

As the bus moved out onto the highway, he stared at the fallow fields and pastures. "I too go to Dallas. In time to celebrate *Los Dias de Los Muertos* with my family."

"What is this Days of the Dead?"

"I'm happy you remember the Spanish I taught you. It is a festival which begins the last day of this month." He held up three fingers. "For three days we honor death and the dead ones."

"Happy Halloween," I said.

"No, it is not the same."

I leaned my head against the window and closed my eyes while Vic rattled on about the Days of the Dead. As I drifted into sleep, I heard him singing softly of bandits and white scorpions in the mountains of Durango.

\*\*\*

I paused outside the white frame house of my childhood on Lanoue Street, studying the chain link fence veiled with honeysuckle vines, the gardenia bushes, the concrete porch with its chipped edge. I looked up at the belly of a 747 on its roaring descent into Love Field. Shaking off the sensory overload, I walked inside.

My father sat in his Lazy Boy, staring at the television. Mother was wiping off the dining room table. When she saw me, a choking sound came out of her mouth as she tried to say my name. She pressed the dishtowel against her mouth as if she wanted to keep something inside, then she hurried over and embraced me.

"You're home at last!" she said, rubbing fiercely at the tears on her cheek. "Justin, Oh, Justin!"

My father rose slowly from his chair, shuffled over and wrapped his strong arms around us. The sound of their weeping tore my guts out.

"Hey," I said. "It's alright. You knew I'd make it out okay." I glanced around the room. "Where's Jimmy and Shelby? I thought you said they'd be here."

They wailed louder. It was an hour before they had the control to tell me what had happened. The next day I booked a flight to Guadalajara.

\*\*\*

On Highway 15 outside of Culiacán, the bus stopped at a ranch and discharged three passengers—men speaking an Indian dialect and wearing cowboy hats, serapes, cotton pants, and *huarache* sandals. As I watched them walk toward the ranch house, I heard several bursts from an automatic rifle.

The man next to me was reading a Guadalajara bilingual newspaper. He didn't seem to notice the loud gunfire.

"Who is firing the machine gun?" I asked.

He glanced up from his paper. "*Los narcos*," he said, and with his lips he made like he spat. He glanced at the copy of Fodor's *Mexico* in my lap. "You are American? You are sightseeing?"

"I'm going to Culiacán," I said.

"Culiacán is my city. We do not often see *Americanos*. Except for our eighteenth century cathedral, there is little that tourists want to see. Why do you travel there?"

"I'm going to ship the bodies of my brother and his fiancée back to the states. They were murdered there last week."

He nodded. "I am sorry for your loss," he said, then lit a cigarette and lost himself in the newspaper.

At the bus station in Culiacán, I took a cab to the home of Rafael Gonzales, a reporter for *Noroeste*, Culiacán's newspaper. The American consulate in Guadalajara knew Rafael personally and had persuaded him to help me transport Shelby and Jimmy back to the states.

Stepping out of the cab, I followed a trail of yellow marigold petals strewn from the road to the scrolled-iron gate in front of the modest stucco house. The wrought iron fence on either side of the gate was connected to high concrete block walls marking the property line. Above the wall to my left, I saw the blackened windows of a neighbor's two-story house. I rattled the gate and called out, "*Señor Rafael Gonzales, por favor!*"

The dark oak door of the house opened, and a man stepped out. He scanned the street both directions before he looked at me.

"*Señor Rafael Gonzalez?*" I asked.

"Yes."

"I'm Justin."

"Ah, yes. Please, come inside. You are welcome here."

I opened the gate and walked through the concrete front yard toward the porch. The yard was carefully landscaped with benches and pots and raised beds in which were planted gardenias, poinsettias, orange and avocado trees. Rafael shook my hand and motioned me inside.

"I trust your trip was without incident?" he said.

"It's not like being on an American bus, but at least it didn't break down. I heard Mexican busses are bad to do that."

He laughed. "Sometimes our busses deserve their reputation." He led me by the arm to the *sala*, the family living room, where several family members stood on the tessellated tile floor. "Justin, allow me to present my family. My wife, Veronica; my son, Miguel; my daughter. Raquel; my mother, *Señora* Gonzales; and my wife's brother, Earnesto."

"*Con mucho gusto,*" I said.

The adults smiled, and the two children, both in their early teens, giggled—I guessed because of my accent. Vic had taught me functional Spanish in Huntsville, but learning Spanish from that Tex-Mex is a lot like learning English from a redneck.

"It is our pleasure, sir," Miguel said in perfect English.

Rafael placed his hand on my shoulder. "This is Justin. The occasion that brings him our way is unfortunate, but he will be our guest this week. Justin, let us sit and talk a moment."

We moved to a red velvet sofa in front of the fireplace. Rafael's wife, mother, and daughter excused themselves and withdrew into the kitchen. Miguel retired to his room, and Earnesto, who wore a police uniform, sat in a chair in front of a desk cleaning a small pistol. When Rafael looked at him, he sighed, rolled his eyes, nodded, loaded the pistol and slipped it into a desk drawer.

Next to the desk, a small rectangular table had been converted into an altar. On the white tablecloth sat three framed photographs surrounded by flowers, burning candles, candy skulls, chocolate skeletons and miniature *maraipan* coffins, a pack of cigarettes, a glass of water, a bottle of tequila, and an oval loaf of sweet bread.

"The *ofrenda* is beautiful, is it not?" Rafael asked.

"Yes. The first such altar I've seen."

"Ah, come and take a closer look."

We rose and walked to the altar.

"Justin, have you ever celebrated *Los Dias de los Muertos*?"

"No," I said. "But a friend of mine told me a little about it. In America, this time of year we observe Halloween."

"Our feast has none of the terror Americans like to attach to Halloween. We use the time to reflect on those who have died, and we seek to come to terms with our own certain death." One by one, he lightly touched each photograph. "My father, my wife's mother. The little one is my sister who died when she was very young. Now she is one of the *angelitos*. Every year, I tell my children about them, things they did not know before—their favorite foods, jokes they played on others, things they said, how they died. It is important to remember the dead. My father often said the dead die only when they die in our hearts."

Rafael picked up the photo of his father. "My father was a journalist as I am. He was assassinated in Mexico City. Journalism in Mexico can be a very dangerous occupation. But he believed that one courageous soul could make a difference. Do you think one man can make a difference, Justin?"

"I don't know. I'd like to think so," I said, looking at Rafael. His face was young, but his dark eyes were the weary eyes of an old man, like the eyes of the hard priest in Texas who had known me in confession all my life.

A painting of a skeletal lady wearing a plumed hat was hung above the fireplace. I pointed to it. "Who is she?" I asked. "Not another relative I hope."

Rafael laughed. "She is death, *La Katarina*, the beautiful lady of our feast. She visits each of us when it is time to die—sometimes violently, sometimes she comes as softly as a whisper. My son has written many *calaveras*, many poems and songs about *La Katarina*. Would you like to hear one?"

"Sure."

"Miguel, *ben aqui*," he called out.

His son ran to us from his room, a *calacas* in his hands. He raised the skeleton and pulled a string that caused it to smile and flap its arms and legs as if it were dancing.

"Sing us the song you wrote for the holiday," Rafael said.

"*¿En Español o Inglés?*" Miguel said.

"*Inglés.*"

Miguel closed his eyes and sang out:

> *I danced with death and did not know her,*
> *And the out-of-tune violin*
> *Played on through the night*
> *To a song that had no end.*
> *And as we danced, I wondered,*
> *When would the music end?*
> *She said, "This dance will last until*
> *You fall, like other dying men."*
> *She had soft hands and a pretty face,*
> *She whispered secrets in my ear,*
> *Her eyes looked deep inside my heart,*
> *And she shed a single tear.*
> *A warm embrace she gave me,*
> *And the world began to spin,*
> *Her fingers reached for my hand,*
> *The fate of dying men.*

When we applauded, Miguel bowed.

"You've got a talented boy," I said.

Rafael lifted the boy's chin and smiled affectionately. "Yes, we are very proud."

"Papa, may I turn on the radio?" Miguel asked.

"Yes, but not too loud."

Miguel ran to the stereo and turned it on. He talked to the *calacas*, whose bony arms and legs danced wildly to the beat of the music as he pulled the strings.

"I saw some kids playing with those skeleton toys at the airport," I said.

"The toys entertain, but they also teach. In Mexico, we want a child's first acquaintance with death to be a cheerful one."

"I try not to think about death."

"Ah, but she thinks of you," he said.

Rafael's wife and daughter returned to the *sala* with a tray of coffee, Coca-Colas, and cookies. Earnesto left his corner chair and joined us in front of the fireplace for the evening *merienda*.

"I am sorry for the loss of your brother and his fiancée," Rafael said. "*¡Que en paz descansen! Es muy triste*, very sad. It must be a great burden to bear, and attending to the details of death requires more strength than many have."

"I've got the strength," I said. I tapped my fingers on the sofa arm to the beat of a song on the radio.

Rafael placed his hand on top of mine and pressed my fingers down so that they ceased their tapping. "When your Spanish has improved, you will not enjoy this song. It's called, '*La Piñata,*' a *corrido,* a ballad about a drug lord's party where bags of cocaine were stuffed into a piñata. A song about a man very much like the man who murdered your brother."

"You know who killed Jimmy?"

"Yes. Would you like to know?"

"Yes, I would."

"Veronica, bring me my briefcase." Rafael leaned back on the sofa. "He is a drug dealer. Unfortunately, in the minds of many, the drug lords are like your famous Robin Hood. They throw people money because they love to be seen as generous benefactors who help the poor. Across from the capitol is a shrine devoted to Jesus Malverde, a *narco* who came from this area. On the same street is a chapel dedicated to his memory. Throughout Mexico we have monuments and songs dedicated to lawless men who steal girls from the poor barrios and kill anyone who asks too many questions or who tries to stop them. Once the Mariachis sang of love, the family, love of our land. Now . . . things are very different."

Veronica brought Rafael a leather attaché. He opened it and searched through the papers until he found a photograph. "This is the man—Roberto Cruz de la Cruz."

I took the photo and held it in my palm. Earnesto leaned over to take a look, raised his eyebrows, and shook his head.

"He's smiling," I said. "A man who kills people I love and smiles."

"He believes he has much to smile about. Not long ago, he was just a local thug. Now, he is the leader of his own organization. And his status and brutality grows every week. Did the consulate tell you the circumstances of their death, how he killed them?"

"No, I don't know any details."

"Earnesto showed me a copy of the police report. Your brother entered a cantina which Cruz de la Cruz frequents every evening. Your brother spoke Spanish very well, so Cruz de la Cruz assumed that he was with the DEA. De la Cruz and his men took them to a hotel room where they were raped, beaten, and tortured with ice picks. The police found the girl nude, on the floor with her back against the bed. Her arms were stretched out and nailed to the posts of the headboard. Your brother's face was stuffed into the toilet."

The images knotted up my insides. "What cantina did they go to?"

"A small one near the plaza."

"What are the police going to do?"

He glanced at Earnesto. "What the authorities usually do here when *los narcos* commit a crime—nothing."

"*Con permiso*," Earnesto said. He stood, snatched a Coke from the tray, and walked outside to the patio.

"Did he understand us?" I asked.

"He does not speak English, but he recognized Crus de la Cruz's photograph, so he knew what we spoke about."

Veronica came to Rafael and placed her hand on his shoulder. "It is time to go to the cemetery," she said.

Rafael took her hand and kissed it. "Of course. The time had escaped me. Come walk with us to the cemetery, Justin."

I followed the Gonzales household outside. Many other families were on the streets, walking and laughing together. Fireworks filled the sky. A parade of singing, costumed people passed us, led by a skeleton with a violin. Following him were skeletal grooms arm in arm with ghoulish brides, ghosts, mummies, and four men carrying a coffin containing a smiling corpse to whom people tossed oranges, flowers, and candy. Mummers followed the coffin, wildly shouting and running about in pursuit of the stubborn dead souls attending the feast.

In the cemetery, families gathered around altars constructed near the graves of ancestors and loved ones. Almost every grave was elaborately decorated with colored paper and arches of flowers. In the flickering light of thousands of candles, the cemetery seemed alive, and the heady aroma of the flowers mingled with the distinctive fragrance of copal incense. A priest moved from tomb to tomb praying for the souls of the departed. When we reached the freshly repainted tombs of Rafael's father and sister, Earnesto lit several candles and votives and placed them on the vaults. With an arm around each child, Rafael told us stories about his father and sister while Veronica laid out a *mole* dish and tamales. After we ate, Rafael opened a bottle of tequila and he poured each adult a generous portion and we toasted the dead. Several toasts and stories later, the bottle of tequila was empty.

A mariachi band made its way through the cemetery playing the favorite songs of the deceased. When they reached Rafael's family, he requested a tune, tipped them, and they began a ballad. The song was slow, waltz-like, with a sad tone. Rafael danced with his wife, Earnesto with Rafael's mother, and Miguel danced with his sister.

I watched for a few minutes, then strolled alone through the cemetery. Stopping for a moment to listen to another mariachi band, I felt a soft hand on my arm. I turned and looked into the black-pearl eyes of a beautiful young woman. She wore a white cotton dress and her long dark hair was pulled tightly back.

She slid her hand from my arm into my hand. *"Baila conmigo."*

*"Con mucho gusto.* I would love to dance," I said and placed my hand on her waist. When I took uncertain steps to the music, she took the lead, gracefully swirling me about.

"You have sadness in your eyes," she said.

Her English surprised me. I didn't know exactly what to say or how to say it, so I only nodded.

"Things will be okay," she said. "What do you call yourself?"

"Justin. And you, what is your name?"

"Catrina," she said. "Is this not beautiful—the lights, the flowers, the families? I am sure the *angelitos* are happy."

When the song ended, we applauded the band and she embraced me. "Thank you for the dance," she whispered in my ear. "*Vas a verme una vez mas.*"

I watched the mariachis stroll on to the next family, and when I turned to talk to the girl, she was gone. I walked back to my friends. Rafael stood behind Veronica with his arms around her waist.

"My new friend," he said. "Did you have a pleasant walk?"

"Yeah, I did. I met a girl and we danced. She was a beauty, too."

"Where is she?"

"I don't know, but she said she'd see me again."

\*\*\*

At dawn, we returned to Rafael's home. I fell into bed, my head buzzing from tequila. A tapping noise woke me later that morning. I sat up in my bed and watched two hummingbirds hover near the window. I put on the robe and rubber flip-flops Vernoica had laid out for me, pulled a towel from my suitcase, and walked to the shower stall in the small open-air wash area. After I showered and dressed, I joined Rafael and his family on the patio for a breakfast of eggs, fried potatoes, corn tortillas, beans, and coffee.

After breakfast, Rafael drove me to the police station where I presented the transit permit and consulate letter. At the funeral home, I obtained the death certificates, proof of embalming, and letters of no contagious disease that I would need at the airport. Rafael and I followed the funeral director's hearse to the airport, and there I presented my papers and signed another mountain of forms. The sealed steel crates holding Jimmy's and Shelby's bodies were loaded onto a plane, and then Rafael drove us to his office. After he had parked, he glanced at his watch.

"I have an important deadline, so I must do some work in my office. You do not need to wait for me. You may take my car if you wish."

"No thank you. I'll just walk around town for a while. I'll take a cab to your home later."

I left Rafael and strolled through Culiacán. At the plaza, I sat on a bench in the shade. Monarch butterflies covered many of the trees around me, and it seemed as if the limbs were full of orange flowers. Occasionally, the wind or noise would stir them and they rose above the plaza in clouds of color.

I watched the families and young people of Culiacán as they strolled around the plaza. Across the street, I could see the cantina where Jimmy and Shelby had eaten their last meal.

A pair of young girls passed my bench and I saw they had each other's names embroidered on their jackets. When two boys flirted with them, the girls hissed. Laughing, the boys sat down on my bench. They were eating jalapeño Popsicles.

"Hello. You are American?" one asked.

"Yes. I'm from Dallas, Texas."

"Dallas? It is good. You are wealthy American like J.R.?"

"No."

When a young girl and her mother walked by, the boys called out, "*Oye, Suegra!*"

The girl ignored them, but her mother turned and smiled.

"Is she your mother-in-law?" I asked one of the boys.

"No, no. It is a compliment, a way of saying I would like for her to be my mother-in-law. Do you have a *novia*, a girlfriend?"

"I did meet a girl at the festival last night. I liked her very much, but I haven't seen her today."

"Perhaps you will see her soon," he said.

A small orange cloud hovered above us. I held out my arm and two butterflies lit on my hand.

"Ay!" one of the boys said. "*¡Como estraño!* We think of the butterflies as the returning souls of the dead. Two in the spirit world must be thinking of you."

"Yeah. And I think of them too." I lifted my arm and the butterflies floated into the sky.

I rose and joined the crowd's plaza perambulations, walking for nearly an hour, hoping to see Catrina again. I thought of her soft hands on my arm, the warmth of her breasts pressed against me while we danced. At sunset, I walked toward the capitol. I came upon the Jesus Malverde shrine housed in a large blue metal shed. Inside, there was a gift shop with a large showcase of silver belt buckles, necklaces, key chains, and bottle openers—all bearing Malverde's image. Polaroids and handwritten notes of thanks for miracles were taped to the walls. One glass case, with a flickering candle on its top, contained a tiny pair of crutches and a cast of a child's leg. A handwritten note indicated these items had been donated by a family in Stockton, California. In a corner, a man knelt praying. In front of him lay a baggie of hair and a set of false teeth. I heard him thank Malverde for helping him and his brother survive a San Quentin prison term.

At the door, I read the inscription on a plaque. It had been donated by Roberto Cruz de la Cruz.

As I walked away from the shrine, my anger toward Cruz de la Cruz grew. I remembered a time when a Bachman Lake bully jumped my brother outside a bowling alley in Dallas. I came on him as he was kicking in my brother's ribs. Picking up a two-by-four, I stove his head in. I lifted my brother from the ground and used my T-shirt to wipe the blood from his face. "No one will ever hurt you and get away with it," I promised him.

I had seen men like de la Cruz in Huntsville. Men with no conscience, no insides. Bullies. Men who thought they were invincible. I also saw a few of these bullies who learned they could bleed and die just like the men they victimized and intimidated. "No one, ever," I said to myself.

When I neared the plaza, I flagged a cab and returned to Rafael's house. I directed the driver to wait for me. Inside, I found Rafael's family eating supper on the patio.

"Justin, I was worried. Come join us for supper," Rafael said.

"No thanks. I've already eaten, and I've got a cab outside. I've got to go back to town."

"He's probably going to meet a girl," Miguel said.

On my way out, I passed through the *sala*, opened the desk drawer, and slipped Earnesto's pistol into my pocket. I directed the taxi to take me to the cantina where Rafael said Cruz de la Cruz spent his evenings.

\*\*\*

THE Hispanic next to me wore a braided leather necklace with an attached cameo of Jesus Malverde. I could see the outline of what I supposed was a shoulder holster beneath his linen jacket. He chugged down a Corona, then laid a gold cocaine spoon on the bar's countertop. On the spoon's handle was a nude figurine of a crucified woman. Her eyes and mouth were slightly open and her head was bent forward so that her long hair fell across her face. The man studied the spoon a moment, then tapped it twice with his fingertips. He smiled, then slipped the spoon back into his shirt pocket. He signaled the bartender to bring each of us another beer.

"*Gracias*," I said.

"*De nada*. But it is no necessary to speak Spanish. I speakeh perfect Englis."

"I can see that. You have a beautiful city."

"Ah, you are a *tourista*. To you *Americanos*, any foreign city is beautiful. It is, *come se dice*, 'exotic'? Where are you from in America, my friend?"

"Dallas, Texas. And you? Where are you from in Mexico?"

"From the mountains of Durango, the land of the white scorpion."

"The white scorpion, rare and deadly," I said.

"Is good you know of such things."

"Yeah, I guess." In the background I could hear a *corrido* about some Sinaloan mountain hick. I listened carefully to the words:

> *They say this man is very bad,*
> *Señores, I don't believe it,*
> *Because he is legendary and valiant,*
> *Because of this they are scared of him,*
> *But at the bottom of his soul,*
> *He is a sincere friend.*

"I don't need a friend like that," I muttered as the song ended.

"What?" he said. "You do not like the ballad?"

"Sorry. Just thinking aloud."

Two men entered the restaurant and he stood up. "You must excuse me. My boss has arrived. You know of him?"

I glanced at the mirror and recognized one of the two as Cruz de la Cruz. "No," I said. With my right hand, I reached into the pocket of my trousers and wrapped my fingers around the handle of the five shot Smith and Wesson .38 revolver.

He patted me on the back. "Is good. Is best this way." He signaled the bartender to bring me another beer, threw a hundred-dollar bill on the bar, walked to the pair, and kissed the hand of Cruz de la Cruz.

I sipped my beer and watched as people in the cantina acknowledged Cruz de la Cruz with smiles and handshakes. Cruz de la Cruz motioned one old man over, pulled several folded Franklins from his pocket and handed the wad of bills to him. The man wept when Cruz de la Cruz embraced him. Cruz de la Cruz pointed at a table and he and his men sat down.

*Nothing to it,* I told myself. *Three men. You have five shots in the pistol. Don't miss. Do it and then haul ass.* I drained the beer and walked over to their table.

The man I had talked with at the bar was sitting next to Cruz de la Cruz. "*¿Que quieres, Americano?*"

"I want to speak to *Señor Tonto.*" I pointed to Cruz de la Cruz.

"*¿Mande?*"

He frowned, so I knew he understood me. His eyes shifted to Cruz de la Cruz. I yanked the pistol from my pocket, pointed at the head of de la Cruz, and pulled the trigger.

The hammer snapped loudly on the defective shell. "Shit!" I said and pulled the trigger again. Snap.

The bullets from their guns plowed into my chest, pushing and whirling me back from the table. I heard screaming and shouting as my back and head slammed against the tile floor. I stared at the swirling decoupage of faces above me until my eyes settled on Jimmy and Shelby. Next to my brother stood Catrina. She smiled sadly and held out her hand.

# A Gift from Erin

WHEN THE TRAIN FROM NEW HAVEN STOPPED AT
GREENWICH, FIONA SPOTTED A MAILBOX ON THE TRAIN
PLATFORM. She told the conductor she'd be right back and exited
the train, briefcase and coffee in hand. She dropped a letter addressed
to her sister, Martina, now in Maghaberry Prison in Northern Ireland,
and then walked back to the train.

After returning to her seat, she set her briefcase in her lap, and
drained the Starbucks *café au lait*. She searched the blank eyes of the
travelers waiting on the train platform. All seemed distant, as if they
sought to look through her, beyond her. None appeared to be
policemen. She felt suspicious about one man, but when his eyes met
hers, he indifferently raised his newspaper.

"Wall Street bastard," she whispered. "Just like the Fleet Street
English." She remembered the suited British detective who had
arrested her sister last year in New York's Grand Central Station, then
taken her in handcuffs on the next flight to Belfast. At her trial,
Martina was given a life sentence for her supposed role in a bombing.
When Fionna heard of her sister's extradition, she promptly joined the
IRA and was given the task of raising money in America for guns and
assistance to IRA children whose parents were being brutalized in
British jails. At Yale, she had mounted an effective letter writing
campaign to encourage the many IRA POW's, and this past summer
had gone to Cuba for special training. The result of that training now
lay in her lap—a briefcase full of gelignite, a present for a visiting
British diplomat—a gift from Erin. The Englishman was scheduled to
deliver a speech outside Grand Central Station at two o'clock. Fionna
had been directed to get as close as she could, and at 1:55 p.m., set the
briefcase down and walk away. A pre-set digital timer would ensure
the death of another enemy of Ireland.

She lifted her wrist and looked at her watch. It was only noon. She
should reach Manhattan ahead of schedule.

Across the aisle sat an old man with a long, white beard. Next to
him sat a young girl. The little one held an hourglass, holding it up and
giggling as she watched the sand flow down.

The image brought her grandfather to mind. Fionna had gone to Ireland to visit him one summer at his small farm outside Baliná. One day she helped him in his garden. As he hoed, she followed, scattering seed along the shallow furrow. When they finished planting, her grandfather scooped up a handful of the sandy soil and let it run through his hand. "I am glad you came to see me. I wish Martina could have come."

"She's busy, Da."

"Yes, I'm sure the Irish Republican Army keeps her very busy. But those she has chosen to work with will bring her and our family nothing but grief. Life is too short to give yourself to a cause one cannot win."

Shaking her head to clear away the daydream, she whispered, "We will win this struggle, grandfather, we ourselves."

At Portchester, a young man boarded and sat next to her. "Hello," he said.

*An Irish accent. Christ,* she thought, *these Irish buggers are everywhere.*

After she opened a copy of *An Phoblacht/Republican News,* he said, "An Irish girl, are you?"

"Yes."

"Name's Seamus," he said. "And you?"

"Fionna."

"I come from Ulster. Where is your family?"

"Baliná."

He glanced at the newspaper. "Are you with the IRA?"

"What's it to you?"

"I don't care much for them. They knee-capped my brother with a Black and Decker drill when he wouldn't join."

"I am sorry for your brother, but war always has casualties. Every soldier knows that. Besides, if you want to compare bad treatment, I could tell you of how the British broke my sister's jaw when they arrested her."

"*Sinn Fein* is not an army. They're a bunch of thugs."

"Why don't you fuck off if you don't like my politics. Anyone truly Irish is committed to uniting all of Ireland. Only then will Ireland have peace."

"You're living in a dream-world. The Irish, even Irish-Americans, won't support the IRA anymore. You try to look like noble freedom fighters, but running drugs and guns and killing innocent people with sniping and bombs make you look like terrorists. Anyway, let's change the subject. I don't like arguing with a pretty girl. Where are you going?"

She looked out the window. The train still had not pulled out of Portchester. "To Grand Central Station. I'm going to leave a gift with someone. And you?"

"I'm going to hear the SallyMacs. They're an Irish band from Memphis playing at some reception for an English big-wig."

"He's a British diplomat." Glancing at her wristwatch, Fionna saw the time had not changed since Greenwich. "Damn it," she said. Slipping the watch off her arm, she shook it, then banged it against the window. The second hand still would not move. "My watch has stopped. I've got a deadline, and I don't want to be late. What time do you have?"

"I forgot my watch this morning, Colleen. Sorry."

"Don't call me a Colleen. My name's Fionna." She leaned toward the old man across from them. "Sir, do you know what time it is?"

He shook his head. "But it's always later than we think."

"Shit," she said as she slumped back into her seat. "Crazy old man." Finally the train began moving, and after what seemed an eternity, pulled into Grand Central Station. Seamus left his seat before the train stopped and stood at the door, talking to the conductor. They both turned and looked at Fionna, and Seamus smiled and shouted, "*Erin go bragh!*"

As soon as Fionna stepped out of the train, a Transit Officer stepped in front of her.

"Miss, please come with me," he said.

"What's the problem?"

"I'm sure there's nothing to it, but a passenger complained that you attempted to sell him drugs. We are obligated to check these things out, so please follow me."

He led her to a small room and pointed to a chair. "Have a seat. A female officer will join us in a few minutes."

After several minutes, Fionna said, "Look, I resent this harassment, and I have no intention of being strip-searched. You Americans better wake up and see the rights you're losing."

"I'm sorry, Miss. Things here have changed greatly since 9-11."

"There's an appointment I've got to keep, and you're going to cause me to be late. You better have a hell of a good lawyer." She cursed herself for not bringing her pistol with its silencer. "What time do you have?"

"It's 1:59. What time is your appointment?"

Fionna glanced at her briefcase and laughed. "Two o'clock."

"What's so funny?" the officer asked.

"You've had anti-terrorist training?"

"Yes."

She handed him the briefcase. "So you know what gelignite is. I intended to present this to a British diplomat. It's a gift from Erin and the Irish Republican Army."

"Shit!" he said.

Fionna glanced at her watch. The second hand was now moving.

# Bodies in the Trinity

Evil is a true thing in Mexico. It goes about on its own legs. Maybe
some day it will come to you. Maybe it already has—Cormac
McCarthy, *All the Pretty Horses*

I AM LA LLARONA, AND I WEEP FOR MY CHILDREN. For
centuries of nights I have wandered along the waters throughout
Mexico. And yes, I walk along the banks of your Trinity River. I have
strolled along your Turtle Creek, your Bachman Lake and the other
waters. You are surprised to find me in your country? Do not be. No,
in my lifetime, your land too was once a part of Mexico.

I am a Mexican ghost, born of a desert tragedy. On that dreadful
night, when I realized my lover had abandoned us, I blew out the last
candle I had lit for him and drowned my two little children, damning
myself forever. But as I was a whore in the eyes of all, what else could
I have done? I had given this man my virginity, my honor, my future.
No one would help us—-not my parents, not the Holy Church, not the
residents of our pueblo. I am forever lost now—in the night, in the
madness, pain, hopelessness, grief, and loneliness. *Ay, mis hijos,
¿Donde Estan mis hijos?*

But I have found I am not so alone.

One night, I came upon a couple--shouting, fighting. Two young
children clutched each other nearby, watching. A boy and a girl. They
so reminded me of my own.

"Jorge, please, take us home," the woman said. "The children are
frightened."

The man spat at her and threw her to the ground. "No. I do not
care where you go, but you will not return with me." He cursed, then
stormed out of sight.

When I came to her, she was weeping. "Why do you weep,
*querida*?" I asked. She shook her head and did not answer, wiping
fiercely at the tears on her cheeks.

I lifted her chin with my hand so she would look at me. "What is
your name?"

"Veronica."

"He was your man, was he not? And now he has left you? Answer me."

"Yes. But who are you? Are you an angel?"

"Yes, *querida.* I am your angel tonight—your guide and guardian."

"Oh, thank you!"

She clutched my legs and buried her tear-stained face in my dress. Her weeping tore my heart.

"Jorge has abandoned me. And now who will take care of my children?" She clenched her fists and held them against her face.

I sat next to her and wrapped my arms around her. "I will help you take care of them. I am your sister. Do you not see the resemblance?" I brushed my fingers through her long dark hair and looked deep into the black-pearl eyes. "I understand your pain. Look into the river. The river holds the secret. The river will tell you what to do."

Dipping my hand into the water, I held my arm up and watched the drops slip back into the river. As she sobbed and stared at the water, I held out my hands to the children. "Come, *hijos.*" I led them back to Veronica, and we sat together, staring at the river. In the distance I could see the Dallas skyline, and even in our remote location, the sirens, and sounds of the city roared in my head. I knew what the mother would soon do, and so I kissed each of them and left them there by the water, and followed Jorge.

I found him leaning against a tree smoking. He smelled of tequila and beer. I stepped behind him and gently tapped him on the shoulder. Turning, he said, "Jesus, you scared me. *Buenos noches.*" He attempted to walk away, but I moved in front of him.

"Ah, but you would not leave me so soon? And such a handsome man." I stroked his cheek and placed my hand on his chest. "Such very fine clothes. Surely you are able to give a woman all the things she needs."

"So the lady wants something from me, tonight, eh?"

I leaned over and kissed him on the cheek and put my arms around his neck. "I knew a man very much like you once. Why are you here, *guapo,* my handsome one? You are all alone and along sad waters."

"I'm looking for a beautiful woman like yourself."

I could see the lust in his eyes. "Why won't you marry Veronica?"

He pushed me away. "You know her, don't you? She sent you? Does she think she can trick me into keeping her? Why should a successful man marry beneath himself? My family disproves of her. As they would of you."

The arrogance in his eyes enraged me. "But she will have nothing without you."

"She is no longer my concern."

"I know you, Jorge, and many more like you." I clutched him and kissed him hard, biting his lip.

"So the lady wishes to play hard?"

"You have no idea how hard I can play." I took him by the hand toward the river. "Come, lie with me."

He grinned. "You will not forget this night."

"Nor you," I said.

He struggled to live, but it was in vain. In those last moments, when I held his head under the water, I knew his thoughts. *How can a woman be so strong? Will my body be found tomorrow in the dirty water of the Trinity?*

You think I'm cruel. A murderer of my own children. A malevolent spirit. Perhaps. But I am no more cruel than your society, which drowns your little ones in violence, in drugs, in neglect. It is a terrible thing to lose a child. If you listen in the quiet of the night, you will hear me weep for my children, and for yours. They are all my children now. I want to save them, but I don't know how. *Ay, mis hijos, mis hijos. ¿ Donde estan mis hijos?* And Dallas has many drowning children for me to cry for.

# Ghost Fires

Sheridan leans against the large conifer to catch his breath and seek relief from the icy, septic claws of the wind. Whenever the wind changes directions, he moves around the tree adjusting to the new attack. As the nylon surface of the Eddie Bauer goose-down parka rubs the tree's rough surface, Sheridan, blank-faced, watches the brittle bark crumble and fall to the indifferent snow. The relentless, moaning wind pushes him in a circular dance around the tree, and a cloud of swirling snow powder engulfs him. He holds the microcassette recorder close to his mouth so that the wind-sounds do not overpower his voice. The metal and plastic surface of the recorder scrapes the bristles of a new beard and a sore on his frostbitten face. The ghost fires of the Aurora borealis dance above him, dance sadly, and the iridescent colors evolve and twist into eerie, chaotic patterns, images that disturb and distract him.

Sheridan holds up the recorder and stares at the slowly turning reels through red and watery eyes. He shakes his head, lowers the recorder to his mouth, and resumes his diary. How did he get here? Sheridan strains to remember, and wills himself to talk, to sift through layers of jumbled memories.

***

He was a history major in the graduate class of his favorite professor, a beautiful Chippewa, who taught Native American literature at the University of Minnesota. Sheridan thought her incredibly intelligent, and a striking lady, especially when she pulled her straight, shoulder length black hair behind her ear, crossed her arms, and leaned against the wall in her favorite lecture position. The silver jewelry she liked to wear jingled softly whenever she gestured and sparkled when light hit the rings and bracelets at the right angle. In class, she frequently flashed a smile Sheridan's way, and would often thank him for his comments. She lectured with intensity as her dark eyes searched the faces of her students and challenged their apathy and ignorance of things Indian. One day Sheridan flipped through a

Reader's Digest coffee table book on the Indians of North America and he came upon a word that caught his attention.

"Can you tell me anything about the Windigo?" he asked after a class lecture about the Cree.

"Many Cree today still believe in the Windigo," she said. "These spirits are invisible, and the most terrifying creatures of the northern forest. The Cree describe them as superhuman beings, thirty feet tall, with slavering, lipless mouths, and hearts of ice. These spirits have an insatiable appetite for human flesh. No man-made weapon can destroy them, and only the most powerful of shamans can provide protection against them. The Windigo begin stalking the forest in search of lone hunters at the onset of winter and flee north at spring."

A week later Sheridan met with his instructor in her office.

"I'm considering writing a thesis on the Cree legends. And to help my research, I'm going to take a winter camping trip to northern Saskatchewan. I've always wanted the winter experience of the northern lights, and I think the solitude will lend perspective to my writing about the Cree myths."

"I'm impressed, Sheridan. It's really quite a creative idea. A trip like that should be quite illuminating and give you many insights into the Cree hunter's mind. I'd like for you to share your experience with the class when you return. It is a good quest."

Quest. The word hit one of Sheridan's mental buttons, and he saw himself as a man on a quest and even imagined writing a best seller based on his experiences and research entitled, *A Hunter of Legends in the Land of the Cree*. The next day, his instructor shared Sheridan's idea with the class.

When the class took a break, one student said, "So, you're going to search for the wily Windigo, Sheridan?" He said this loudly, and the slobber he allowed to run down his pocked face added to the effect of his sarcasm and the other students in the class howled with laughter.

"You are such a brown noser."

"Piss on you, Brad. I don't know how a moron like you could even get into a graduate program. Try being serious about something for once."

Sheridan prepared for the trip carefully. He read every book he could find on winter camping and studied several issues of *Backpacker Magazine*. John, a friend who owned a sporting goods store, sold him his equipment, taught him to use a compass and topographic maps, and demonstrated how to walk in snowshoes. When Sheridan explained his thesis idea and how he wanted to view and experience the land through the eyes of a lonely Cree hunter, John frowned thoughtfully but nodded as he placed a red, plastic, square sign on the store's stuffed grizzly, its mouth frozen in a permanent snarl. The sign advertised a sale on wilderness survival kits.

"Well," he said, "You've picked a harsh area to camp in. Going alone, you'll experience the loneliness—and more."

Sheridan flew into Prince Albert in northern Saskatchewan and rented a four-wheel-drive Subaru station wagon. He drove to the Canadian police station on Highway 905. From the station, he planned to go north until he reached Lake Deception, then go southwest until he reached an abandoned Hudson Bay outpost, then he could circle back to the highway. He estimated the total distance of his trek to be no more than ten miles. He guessed one could walk at least five miles a day on snowshoes, and concluded he could easily complete the trek in a week.

No one was at the station. After waiting for two hours in the gravel parking lot, he assumed that the Mounties were out on business. He left a note on his vehicle detailing his itinerary, loaded up his red toboggan, and hiked north from the station into the Canadian forest toward Lake Deception.

Hiking on snowshoes was much more physically demanding than he had expected, and the thrill of adventure quickly waned. After only a few hours of walking, his legs ached and cramped, his eyes were irritated from the caustic wind, and his head hurt. He stopped for a moment to jot down some notes. He pulled his small writing pad and pen out of his parka pocket. When he removed his mitten, his hand stiffened immediately in the icy wind. When he tried to write, he discovered the cold had thickened the ink, so he tossed the useless pen into the snow. He dug around in his pack until he found a pencil. After he had written a couple of lines, the point broke. He opened his pocketknife, but his hand shook so badly that he couldn't sharpen the pencil. He gave up on the idea of writing anything and walked on. Everything, even the smallest of tasks, seemed so complicated here--in the hungry land of the Windigo. An hour later, exhausted, he pitched his tent, climbed in his sleeping bag, and fell into a deep sleep.

After six hours of hiking on the second day, he neared a creek bottom and heard an approaching snowmobile. As the black Skidoo topped a hill, Sheridan observed how it sped along smoothly over the same snow he had fought with to the point of exhaustion. The snowmobile carried two passengers and towed a toboggan bearing a large buck. A young boy sat behind the adult driver. A white dusting of snow covered their red wool coats. When they spotted Sheridan, they drove into the creek bottom and killed the engine. The moaning and whistling sounds of the wind quickly replaced the sewing machine noise of the two-stroke engine. The pair lifted their arms in greeting, and waited patiently for Sheridan to trudge down to them. By their dark hair and skin, Sheridan thought they must be Indians.

"Hello. You are far from the road. You are hunting also?" The voice of the father sounded warm, and the English better than Sheridan had expected.

"Not a hunter of animals. I am doing research for the University of Minnesota."

The father nodded and said, "My son and I were going to stop and build a fire. We would be happy to share our food with you." The Indians stared at his snowshoes and toboggan.

"Thank you," he said, panting. "I am ready for a break myself, and I could use some company."

The father took the Remington bolt-action rifle slung on his back, laid it on the snowmobile, turned to his son, and said, "Gather some wood."

The boy made two trips to some nearby trees and broke off armfuls of dead branches, which he brought to his father. The father removed his mittens, stacked the sticks in a teepee shape on an exposed rock, and used a cigarette lighter to start the fire. He stood up, dusted some snow from his ragged wool coat, and nodded to the boy who kneeled down and steadily fed the small fire larger sticks until they had a good bed of coals. The father then stepped to the snowmobile and picked up a burlap bag from which he removed a square foil package. He unwrapped it and dropped the frozen square into a pan and dropped it on the coals.

The pre-cooked venison stew quickly thawed, and the aroma made Sheridan's mouth water. The spoons scraped the side of the aluminum bowls as the stew filled and warmed Sheridan's stomach, and he thought it tasted much better than the MRE's, oatmeal, and granola bars in his pack. The sun vanished, and they found themselves under the stars of a beautifully brilliant Arctic sky. Orion, the hunter, majestically dominated the portion of sky in Sheridan's frame of vision. The stars sparkled in the clear sky and reminded him of the silver jewelry on his professor's arm which flashed with every gesture in the warm, sunlit classroom.

After the meal, the boy fetched a battered Stanley thermos and tin cups, and poured each a steaming cup of coffee. Sheridan reached into his pack and pulled out a fifth of Crown Royal he had brought along for special moments. He poured a good dose into their cups, and then turned on the microcassette recorder. He thought the moment a perfect opportunity to gather information about Indian legends.

"Tell me about yourselves. Where do you live? How often do you hunt out here?" he inquired. He drank down his coffee quickly, and the edge of the tin cup burned his lip and the coffee scalded his tongue.

"We are Cree, and we now live on the reservation. Sometimes my family lives in Prince Albert when there is work. Some of my cousins are steel workers and have moved to New York. During the winter, my son and I often take hunting trips. I have never seen one . . . like yourself—walking and camping alone in the winter. Where are you going?"

"I am looking for Lake Deception. Do you know if I am close?"

"There are many lakes in Saskatchewan, but I do not recognize such a name. You should go back."

"Maybe you know the lake by an Indian name?" Sheridan was puzzled; the map showed the rather large body of water to be somewhere in this locale. Sheridan was also somewhat disappointed in the Indians. Not only because they didn't know their geography, but they did not resemble the image of Indian hunters his professor had created in class. Much too modern. Sheridan briefly took a mental side trip and imagined the same father and son living as the Cree did a hundred years ago: when they spoke Cree instead of English; took long hunting treks across the subarctic to return with bundles of furs which they would trade to the Hudson Bay outposts for guns, beads, and whiskey; when the Cree families lived in smoke-filled birch bark homes; and gnawed leather in the worst winters because there was no food. He served himself and the father more whiskey. After the Crown kicked in, Sheridan questioned the father about the legend of the northern lights that flashed and swirled above their heads.

"My ancestors believe these lights to be the camp fires of lost spirits, doomed men who died in battle or alone on hunting trips. Now, these warriors—sad, lonely, and lost—are nomad spirits who must forever travel the dark skies above the cold land of the Cree."

Sheridan was impressed with the eloquence and heartfelt emotion of the father's speech. His son nodded to his father's words as he occasionally added another stick to the fire. Sheridan, excited, stared at the northern lights as the father spoke, and for a moment imagined he actually saw a Cree warrior spirit on the border of the horizon stumbling and weaving his way toward them.

"Tell me about the Windigo," he said.

"It is bad luck for hunters to talk about the hungry spirits. If you even mention their name, they come hunting for you," the Indian whispered. Something in his tone changed. The Indian swept his arm toward the shadow filled forest. "There are many of them, and they feed on lone hunters. Sometimes one can hear them fighting among themselves in the woods. The trappers have left, our people now live on reservations, only the hungry spirits remain. We need to return home now." He glanced nervously toward the woods, abruptly turned to his son, and spoke sharply in an Indian dialect. Without another word to Sheridan, they packed up and sped away on the snowmobile, the buck in tow, his frozen legs straight up in the air. Sheridan stared at the fire as the sound of the machine faded and its lights vanished in the darkness. As the boy had done, Sheridan fed the small fire an occasional stick. He realized that he must have committed a *faux-pas* when he asked the Indian about the Windigo. Nothing like ruining a good conversation. Their reaction revealed how slowly Stone Age superstition dies. Maybe later he could take a trip to the Cree reservation and arrange some interviews with the less reticent and more enlightened of the tribe. Sheridan put up his tent, crawled into its protection, and slept.

After an oatmeal breakfast and cups of tea, Sheridan broke camp. He marked his estimated location on the topographic map, set his compass, and waddled and shuffled awkwardly through the snow. Sheridan did not understand why he could not find Lake Deception. Maybe the lake was covered with snow and he had unknowingly walked over it. Perhaps he had figured the compass declination incorrectly. If he had made a significant declination error, he might not even be close to where he wanted to go. His stomach churned.

Sheridan decided to return; the trek had nothing more to add to the thesis. He had experienced the harshness of the Cree's land sufficiently to write with understanding and empathy. The decision made, he set his course south, hoping to find the way back to his starting point at the Mountie station or at least to the highway.

Sheridan walked on until exhaustion set in. He set up the Eureka four-season tent and for comfort more than warmth, built a small fire on an exposed rock. He heard wolves in the distant darkness in between the roaring gusts of the demon wind. Sheridan crawled into his tent, and slept an hour until the silence awoke him. He glanced outside the tent and saw that dark clouds had rolled in and the air felt warm and humid.

Before long, the snow began. Big flakes drifted slowly to the earth. Sheridan unzipped the top section of the tent door and wrapped in the down sleeping bag, watched the snow fall for a half-hour. As the snowfall thickened, visibility shrank to a few yards. Sheridan decided to wait the storm out. He zipped up the tent door but left a small open for ventilation. The heat of his butane lantern made the tent almost comfortable. He lay down and had just dozed off when he heard some growls outside the tent, followed by snapping, popping sounds. Sheridan guessed that some wolves fought over supper—a deer, rabbit, or some other unlucky creature of the northern woods. Maybe fifty yards away, but distance and location were difficult to measure with certainty in this country. A man from Ontario once told him that pilots often crashed in the North Country in whiteouts or even on the gray winter days because there was no clear horizon. Unable to distinguish between the ground and sky, between what was real and what was hallucination, the pilots lost their bearings. Sheridan opened the flap of the tent, and strained his eyes to scan the area around the tent and thought he saw the dark shadow-shapes of wolves move through the tree line on a nearby ridge. Sheridan lay down, slept, and dreamed of the warm Louisiana swamp he once hunted and camped in as a young boy.

When Sheridan awoke again, so much snow had piled up that he had to leave the tent and use a snowshoe to dig away snow from the top and entrance of the tent. Finally, the snow stopped, but gale force winds followed. When Sheridan went to his food bag hanging in the branches of a nearby tree, he found it on the ground, most of its contents eaten and trampled. He thought he had put it high enough to keep animals out of it. Frustrated and hungry, Sheridan poured the last of his fuel into the stove and lantern, finished the bottle of Crown, and realized he didn't have many moments of heated comfort left. The wind steadily grew in intensity, and angrily whipped the tent with its gusts, as if it were a creature that wanted to rip through the thin fabric. Even with his lantern's heat, the cold seeped deep into his bones, and his teeth chattered constantly. Some lines from Milton's descriptions of hell flashed in mind. "Beyond this flood a frozen Continent. . . Thaws not. . . all else deep snow and ice. . . cold performs th' effect of Fire. . . fierce extremes. . . to starve in Ice. . ." Sheridan cursed his luck, cursed the weather and recorded some ideas for a personal essay entitled: "My Journey into the Hell of the Cree in Search of the Windigo."

When he heard more growls and cracking noises, Sheridan again looked outside the tent, but could see nothing. He decided to break camp. The station and highway could not be far away; he resolved to walk until he reached something civilized. Sheridan dug his frozen tent from its icy vault and loaded it onto his sled.

Sheridan jerked the toboggan and began the monotonous and exhausting hike again. His eyes burned from the brightness of the snow and the wind. Each time the malicious talons struck his face, he felt as if someone poked at his eyes with an ice pick.

The darkness of this land was surreal. It didn't seem natural for the sun to emerge, skim the horizon, and then disappear so quickly. It unnerved Sheridan to see the few moments of light fade to an aberrant twilight and then shortly find himself dumped again into a choking and extended Cimmerian darkness. Sheridan had heard that a man can go nuts if he stays too long in the dark.

Sheridan felt his body weaken as he walked. He knew he needed food for energy and body heat. Sometimes experience forces redefinition of terms. Sheridan decided that hunger is not the minor discomfort one feels when a meal or two is missed. Hunger, real hunger, is a creature with beaver-like teeth that hatches and gnaws constantly on your stomach. He reflected on an article in the New Yorker about a doctor who said his experiences in Bosnia documented that one chocolate bar could add eleven more days to a child's life. And he thought about the Antarctic explorers he heard on NPR who said on their trek they ate a pound of butter of day . . . .

***

The recorder clicks and Sheridan lowers it from his face to his side. His arm and back are sore. He rewinds the tape and plays it back, but after a few minutes of rambled journal entries, all he can hear is the wind.

Sheridan tries to count the exact number of days, extending fingers one by one within his mittens, but his numb brain loses count. He can't recall the last time he had eaten or even what day it was. What if he was late to class? What if he was lost? The wind changed directions again and bit his windburned face and snow-blinded eyes like a beast.

"This cold is eating my ass. Christ, how could the Indians have stood this?"

Sheridan hears laughter and a loud hiss. He peers around the conifer in the direction of the sound of crunching snow; he sees a large shadow-like shape streak through the trees a few yards away. Once again, the wind whips across his exposed face, and his eyes water and

83

burn. He concentrates and focuses his vision in the twilight. In his peripheral vision he sees the shape again, only now it is much closer, within a few feet. He jerks around; nothing is there, but he sees bloody footprints in the snow. He pulls off a mitten and fumbles for his knife, his microcassette recorder still in his left hand. The wind dies and Sheridan feels lost in the silence. Another streak. He wheels again, still trying to find his lock-blade. Again, he hears laughter.

"Playing with me, are you?" He awkwardly attempts to run in the snowshoes. His right jaw suddenly explodes and the force of the blow knocks Sheridan on his back. A cloud of powdery snow flies upwards.

The stars swirl in a tracer-like pattern. He touches his jaw with his right hand; it is wet and warm, covered with blood. Slow footsteps crunch in the snow. More laughter. An Indian, dressed in the old style of caribou skin garment worn by the Cree in the paintings he studied in school, towers above him, a bloody wooden war club in his hand. His lipless face smiles wickedly, and his eyes roll in blood. Sheridan sees the jagged teeth. *Hearts of ice*, she had said. Sheridan closes his eyes to the hallucination. Sheridan orders his tired and weakened limbs to move. They won't. He can still feel his recorder in his left hand and he hears the tape turning. He opens his eyes and can see the multicolored ghost fires dance brightly in the dark sky above him, and the sad, shadowy form of a Cree warrior, the horizon-walker, materializes. He beckons Sheridan with his hand to join him at his campfire. He whispers some words in an Indian dialect, and points toward the horizon. There is a sad, understanding tone in his voice.

As the warrior comes closer, Sheridan sees a scarred face, and leather clothes torn and bloody as though a wild creature had torn and fed on his body. Something cold grabs Sheridan's arm and drags him roughly out of the snowdrift. A large foot rests heavily on his chest, and huge, strong, claw-like hands rip off his parka. The wind whips across his face, torn stomach, and exposed body. Sheridan hears the tearing of his flesh and the crunch and snap of bones as the Windigo devours him . . . .

# A Dark Corner in Dallas

A Doors' song played in his head as Martin strolled slowly in front of the Majestic Theatre in Dallas. No one spoke to him, nor he to anyone. It was close to midnight, but the streets were full of people. Even at this late hour, Dallas still had the bustle of an insomniac city that doesn't like to sleep. He passed a homeless man, on the street so long that no life was left in his eyes, no soul was there. It had been long extinguished by the booze and filth of his existence. He thought about luring him into the alley, but he felt it too early to succumb to his ennui. Better prey would surely present itself. The hunting knife in the pocket of his khakis lay flat against his leg, and it burned, and he longed to feel the knife in his hand, to see its razor edge slide along pale skin, to see the thin red line of blood.

A couple exited the Majestic in front of him. They were drunk, and obviously tourists. The girl giggled at some nonsense and pointed above to the tall buildings above Martin. Her eyes briefly met Martins and she smiled. He returned the smile. She was young, the man a little older than she, perhaps by ten years. He slowed his pace so he could follow them. They stopped and the man withdrew a map from his inside pocket. He passed them, listening to them argue about where they were. He stopped just beyond them and lit a cigarette. Tourists were so predictable.

"Excuse me, sir," the girl said. "Can you tell me if there's an open bar nearby?"

"Oh, yes." he said. "What kind of bar do you prefer?"

"Preferably an after hours club, a place with a classy crowd where we can dance the night away."

"I know just the place. It's rather hard to explain, but you're not far. I was on the way there myself. I'll guide you there if you like."

"Oh that would be so sweet."

"Yes, it will be. Follow me. I know a shortcut."

He led them away from the parking lot where he knew their car would be. "Did you drive to Dallas?"

"Yes."

"You must have a nice car. I drive a Saturn myself."

"We have a Lexis."

"Ah, nice car. I thought about getting one myself." *I'll give yours a test drive later.*

They walked a couple of blocks, then turned left, down an alley. The couple was so engrossed in their necking, that they were oblivious to their surroundings. The naiveté of tourists never failed to surprise Martin. A lone security light hung over one store's rear entry, and he walked toward its smog-encrusted nimbus of yellow light.

"It's dark," the girl's date said.

"Parts of Dallas can be very dark, but one gets used to it. Just walk toward the light."

"I'm glad you're guiding us," she said. "We'd be so lost otherwise."

At the box-end of the alley sat a dumpster. A mangy cat walking on the crown of a splintered board fence, yawed from its course and sprung inside the dumpster and buried itself in the rubbish.

"This is a dead end," the girl said.

"Yes, exactly." He positioned himself between them and the only way out of the alley.

"Come on, Julie, let's get away from this weirdo." The man grabbed the girl's hand and tried to step around him, but when Martin blocked their path, the man pushed him. "You had better get yourself out of our way."

Martin smiled and shoved the man back.

"Gerald, let's just go. Please, mister. Don't cause any trouble."

"Aw, is Julie afraid Gerald might hurt me?" Martin said. His fingers had already wrapped around the handle of the knife. He discreetly slid it from its sheath, and cupped it in his hand, the hilt downward, the blade flat against his forearm.

"Mister," Gerald said, "Get out of our way. I'll give you like two seconds to move before I kick your . . . "

Martin cut the man's throat before he could finish the sentence. The man had not even seen his hands move. The man stood as if paralyzed. Martin tilted his head and contemplated the man's new mouth, a red grin on a businessman's white neck. Martin knew the man was in shock. A big-bladed knife shocks the human system more effectively than a small pistol. The man's hand clutched the red wetness streaming in waves down his body, his eyes rolled, and then he collapsed. The wild-eyed girl froze, like an actor onstage in a tableau. When the peril of her situation came to her, she tried to dash by Martin, but he hooked his arm around her waist and yanked her tight against him. Martin scooped up a rag from the ground and crammed it into her mouth to muffle her screams. She flayed at him with her helpless arms as he dragged her into the dark corner of the alley, into the shadows.

Martin whispered, "Bad things can happen in a dark corner of Dallas, Julie. A lot of bad things." He slowly lifted the knife, extended it so that its bloody blade sparkled in the light just beyond her reach. "It's time we dance the night away, just liked you wanted." Her frantic hyperventilating moans became whimpers, and before he was done, the whimpers faded too. Soon, there was no sound at all.

# Like a Good German Soldier

ONE MAY AFTERNOON I WAS PLAYING WITH MY WORLD WAR II TOY SOLDIERS ON MY FRONT PORCH. I wove jeeps and tanks through elaborate battle-lines of German and American soldiers, and as usual, the Americans gave the Nazis a beating.

My father opened the screen door, stepped onto the porch and carefully maneuvered his way through my battlefield carnage. "Come on, son." He walked toward our next-door neighbor's house.

"Yes, sir." I scooped up my armies and threw them into their cardboard shoebox and trotted after him. Barefoot, I hopped across the sticker-filled scorched grass, taking care not to step in the black-dirt cracks that often served as trenches and bomb craters in my war games.

After he rang the doorbell, a man appeared. He was younger than my father, with a blonde crew cut and ice-blue eyes.

"Yes," he said, with a thick accent I had only heard on *Hogan's Heroes*.

"I'm Amos," he said, "and this is my son, Eugene. We live next door and want to welcome you to our neighborhood."

He smiled and opened the door. "Please, come in, and thank you."

A very young and pretty woman sat at their dining table reading an issue of *Life Magazine*.

"I am Rennicke," he said, "and this is my wife, Erma. We are from Germany—from Dresden."

"I'm from West Texas, myself," my father said. "Eugene here was born in Dallas."

"Please sit at the table and have some refreshments," Erma said.

"That's mighty nice of you," my father replied.

Erma stepped into the kitchen and returned with bottled Cokes and a plate of cookies. My father took a long swallow of the Coke. "Ain't nothing like a cold Coke on a hot day. It gets real hot here in Texas sometimes."

"Dresden could be warm at times as well," Rennicke said.

My father nodded. "Reckon so. I hope you like it here in America. My wife always wanted to see Germany since her grandparents came from there. I had a couple of uncles who saw Germany in World War II. I was drafted the day after the war ended and sent to Alaska."

On the wall hung a picture of a German soldier in military dress. I rose from my chair and stepped closer for a better look.

"That is Rennicke," Erma said. "He was sixteen when that photograph was taken."

"You were a real German soldier?" I asked.

"Yes. Like your father, I was drafted," Rennicke said. "But I did not fight Americans. Germany sent me to the Russian Front. Amos, what duty did you have in the army?"

"They made me a clerk," my father replied.

"I was a photographer." Rennicke stepped to a bookshelf and picked out a photo album. He laid it on the table and opened it. "See?"

"Cool!" I said. I could hardly believe my luck. A ten-year-old like me getting to meet a real Nazi. And he had war pictures! This was even better than the last neighbor's South American monkey. I scanned the room searching for swastikas and scooted my chair closer to the table so I could have a better look.

Rennicke slowly turned the pages, talking about each picture. Occasionally he asked Erma how to say something in English. Most of the photos were of soldiers marching through deep snow, bombed cities, and battlefields strewn with dead bodies. On the last page, he pointed to two very dead Germans, lying side by side in their greatcoats, their arms stiff and reaching into the air.

"They were my best friends," he said. "We grew up together. We were so young, but we were good soldiers. We knew the war was lost, but what could we do?"

I saw tears in Rennicke's eyes, and Erma reached over and patted him on the shoulder.

My father nodded. "It's always hard on a man to lose a friend."

When our visit ended, my father invited the couple to come over that night to meet my mother, listen to country music, and to enjoy a Mexican dinner. They thanked us and we excused ourselves.

As we walked home, my father said, "I know he was a Nazi, and you know my uncle was killed by one of their snipers, but I reckon we can't hold that against Rennicke and Erma, so you be real nice when you talk to them."

"Yes, sir," I said. As my father ruthlessly punished any mistreatment of people generally, the thought of abusing our Nazi neighbors had not entered my mind. My father's punishments were few, but memorable. At times brutal enough to cause any Gestapo agent to nod in approval.

Later that afternoon, my friend Clifton Ray came over. As usual, he was loaded down with equipment for our war games. He handed me one of his wooden toy rifles with a roll of caps, and we divvied up the dummy grenades he had purchased at the Army and Navy surplus store.

I snatched the German helmet. "I want to be the Germans today."

"Why? You always make me be the Germans," Clifton Ray said.

"I just want to be the Germans today."

"You'll lose."

"I know. This time, let's pretend we're in Russia."

"Where's Russia?" Clifton Ray asked. "Ain't in Mexico is it?"

"I don't know where it is, but it's got lots of snow."

We played until dark, tossing grenades and sniping at each other from prone and standing positions. As mother called for me to come inside and clean up for supper, Clifton Ray jumped from behind the bushes and fired the final bullet of our conflict. I died—dutifully and dramatically—like a good German soldier. Clifton Ray saluted me, gathered up his arsenal, and walked home. The German helmet still on my head, I rose from my imaginary deathbed of snow and saw Rennicke on his front porch with a camera. He took my picture, nodded, and then stepped back into his house.

# Little Rose and the Confederate Cipher

Sacred Hearts Convent, England, 1871

The nuns here taught me that a "cipher" is a dark secret. My life's been filled with dark secrets, and most of them the world will never know, and some of them I'll never understand.

My father died not long after I was born, and I've no memory of him. I was only nine years old when my mother drowned in 1864. She had left England on a blockade runner, but the ship grounded on a sandbar off the coast of Virginia. Fearing capture by the Yankees, she tried to escape, but her rowboat overturned and the Confederate gold she carried dragged her to the ocean's bottom. I still miss Mama, but I don't cry for her like I did. I know I'm not the only child who lost her mama in the war of the South's secession, but it doesn't make losing mine any easier.

Sometimes I dream of the day Mama and I were arrested and sent to Old Capitol Prison. I had just looked out the window. "Lincoln's Pinkerton man is back, Mama," I said.

My mother, also named Rose, had been writing on a small piece of paper. The handwriting was strange to me. Confederate cipher she called it. She set down her reading glasses and dropped the pen into the inkwell. "Tell me what you see, Little Rose."

"He's outside talking with two Yankee soldiers. You want me to open the door?"

I heard the man knocking.

"You know they've come to take me to prison."

I nodded.

"My friends warned me." She blew the blotting sand off the paper and rolled it into a tiny cylinder. "So, I want you to take this. Put in your stocking, and promise me no one will ever see it. Tell me, Little Rose."

"I will never show it to a living soul."

When I opened the door, the Pinkerton man strode past me and said, "Rose Greenhow, you and your daughter are under arrest for treason." He nodded to the soldiers with him. "Search the house."

"You're going to arrest Little Rose too?" mother asked.

"Those are my orders." He grinned cruelly. "As General Sherman said, 'There is a class of people—men, women, and children—who must be killed or banished before we can hope for peace and order. To the secessionist . . .'

"Death is mercy," my mother said. "I know what General Sherman thinks. I've entertained him in this very house. What are you looking for?"

"Information you're intending to pass to the enemy," he replied.

My mother glanced at me and smiled. "You'll find no evidence of that here, sir."I wanted to spit on this man and his guards who had come to arrest my mama. My ill will must have shown on my face because my mother placed her hand on my shoulder and said, "Rosey. Shhh."

Old Capitol Prison was a terrible, dilapidated place. Once it had been a grand boardinghouse where she had been courted by men like Congressman John C. Calhoun. It wasn't grand when I saw it. I still recall the gallows I could see through the iron bars of our window and the others there with us—blockade runners, spies, and Confederate general. There were even newspaper editors from the North who had dared to criticize Lincoln or Stanton or Seward.

We weren't given much food in the five months we were there. Without the help of some of the other prisoners and people on the street who would slip us food, we would surely have starved to death. At times I was so hungry and cold that I would cry myself to sleep on that hard prison bed. I knew my mother was hungry too, but she never complained. She would just pat my back and sing softly to me until I fell asleep. She had a toughness that most mothers don't have.

One day, that Yankee photographer, Matthew Brady, came to Old Capitol Prison and photographed us. I'm told he did it because we were the most notorious Confederate prisoners there, and I guess it means something to be famous like that. Brady's photograph is the only one I have of my mother. The photograph will tell you some things about us, but it won't tell you of the hardships we endured there—the abusive guards, the bugs, the hunger, the cold, nor will it tell you about the cipher in my gray stocking.

Mother never told me what the cipher meant, nor if that little piece of paper was what the Yankees were looking for. I had always meant to ask her about it.

Years later, I stand outside the convent my sister had placed me in when Mama drowned and whispered my goodbye. I sighed and wondered what parts of me had been left in its cold stone walls, my home now for over six years. The nuns had been good to me, tutored me, cared for me, but they couldn't take the place of my mama, the "Wild Rebel Rose." Nor could they take away the anger and pain in my heart. My mama's war had cheated me of my childhood and taken away my mother and sisters. I couldn't decipher why it all had happened to me.

At my sister's house, I retired early and found myself missing Mama. I removed my scuffed shoes and carefully peeled the gray stocking off my foot, waiting for the faded cipher to fall out and float to the floor like it had every night. It didn't. I panicked and quickly turned the stocking inside-out. I realized that the little piece of paper was gone.

The cipher I never understood was lost. Just like my mother. Like my childhood. Just like the lost cause of the Confederacy. But I had kept my promise to my mama. I had never shown that piece of paper to a living soul.

# No Brakes

"Anyone can kill an enemy,
but it takes a strong man to kill a friend."
— Eskiminzin, Apache chief.

Roger had been my best friend for over ten years. He was also movie-actor handsome, a Don Juan able to charm his way into the arms of most women. He had always been energetic and charismatic, conning and charming his way out of tight and awkward situations that would have buried anyone else. Then Roger's luck ran out. He lost his job. After his wife caught him whoring around, the divorce cleaned out his bank account and separated him forever from his kids. Depression set in, his drinking intensified, and I would lose contact with him for weeks at a time whenever he binged and vanished into his whiskey-hazed world. After I read in the paper that he had been busted for writing hot checks, I felt sick to my stomach, wondering where his self-destructive path would end. And then something happened that had never happened before—he called and asked me to bail him out of jail. I found a bondsman and took care of it.

When I woke the next morning after a troubled sleep, I figured it was time for Roger and I to have a heart to heart talk, so I drove to Roger's Oak Cliff address and parked my BMW behind a battered black 62 Ford Fairlane. An older man sat on the front porch of the rundown house. His eyes were tired and jaundiced, his unshaved face grizzled. Like the house, he had obviously seen better times. A bicycle with two large side baskets was upturned and he appeared to be tightening its spokes with a tiny rusted crescent wrench.

When I stepped out of the BMW and walked toward him, he said, "Nice car." He pointed to the Fairlane. "That be my car. Lord, she was fast and sleek, just like my women. She was running good till she lost her brakes. Then it seemed like nothing else would work right. Now I can't even get her started. So I guess she's just going to sit there till she rots or gets towed off."

94

"I guess if you ain't going to fix it, that would be the best thing." I spat into the grass, and then lit a cigarette. "You know a white boy named Roger?" I asked. "He's supposed to live at this address."

"Where you from, cracker?" he asked. He pointed at my cigarettes. "I shore would like one of them Kools."

I shook him out a cigarette and then pitched him a paper book of matches. "I really ain't got time for small talk," I said. "You know this boy Roger or not?"

"Yeah, he be around back." He pointed to his right. "That crackhead lives in the bottom apartment with an outside door. He gots lots of beer cans piled up. I guess he gonna get in the can business too."

"Much obliged," I said.

"A man can make good money pickin' up cans."

"I wouldn't know."

At Roger's door, I heard Jim Morrison's tormented voice singing "The End." I pounded on the door with my fist till Roger answered. His face was drawn and streaked, his hands dirty and scabbed. His movie-star handsome looks were fading fast.

"Oh, hey, Ken. You out slummin?" He grinned as he wiped sleep crud from his eyes. He eyed the Burger King sack in my hand.

"I brought you a meal. Why don't you invite me in? And turn down that damn music so we can talk."

"Sure." He opened the door and motioned me into the cluttered apartment. "Thanks for getting me out of county, Ken. You're a good friend."

"Yeah, a good friend." I scanned the room. A forest of empty beer bottles rose in the midst of overflowing ashtrays and pizza boxes filled with petrified crusts. "It stinks like shit in here, Roger. Why don't you clean it up once in a while?"

"Ah, It ain't so bad. The maid's just falling down on the job."

"You ain't got no maid, no girlfriend either. Probably couldn't even get it up if you could find one that would put up with your sorry ass." I pointed to the glass pipe on the coffee table. "You're burning rock again, ain't you?"

He shrugged his shoulders. "Not much. I got things under

control."

"Crack or ice?"

He smiled, but his face was blank. One eye twitched, and the other crossed strangely.

"Control, shit," I said. "You're strung out. Roger. Look at yourself. You couldn't stop using if you wanted to. "

"Don't start preaching at me, man. I thought you were my friend."

"I am your *best* friend, Roger. That's why I'm here. I'm going to make you stop this shit."

He laughed. "Oh, sure. Ken's going to make me go to rehab?" He sat down on the mildewed couch and ate the burger and fries I had bought him.

When he finished, I sat next to him. I pulled the .38 from my cargo pants pocket and pressed it against his forehead. "Close your eyes, Roger. It's time for rehab."

# Chinde

When the unclean spirit is gone out of a man, he walketh through dry
places, seeking rest; and findeth none.

--Matthew 12:43

EDUARDO STEPPED UP ON A BOULDER AND SCANNED
THE DESERT FOR THE NEXT CAIRN MARKING THE TRAIL.
The heat waves shimmered into the sky from the desert ground and the
distant mountains moved and bent in the refracted air. After he spotted
the cairn, he lifted his straw cowboy hat and wiped his forehead with
the long sleeve of his khaki shirt. He slicked back his shoulder-length
black hair with his hand, and then slid down the boulder. Charles and
Bronwynn, his two fellow hikers, were studying a topographic map
spread on the ground.

"I spotted the next cairn, Charles," Eduardo said. "Shinny up this
rock and take a look. The ice cave is an hour beyond the cairn."

Charles spat dry phlegm from his mouth and took a long drink
from his water bottle. He stepped up on the boulder and scanned the
dark ground surrounding them. "You've got better eyes than I do,
Eduardo. I can't tell which pile of rocks you're talking about."

Eduardo squinted his eyes, focusing on blurred movement in the
brush. A roadrunner battled with a rattlesnake. Both creatures seemed
abnormally dark, their midnight-dark coloration a camouflage in the
rugged volcanic terrain. A strange contrast to what desert visitors
would see fourteen miles south, where the black New Mexico
landscape would give way to white gypsum sands, and there the skins
of the same animals would be abnormally light.

Edward saw Bronwynn shudder when a scorpion scurried past the
toe of her boot.

"God, even the scorpions are black here," she said. "It's so damned
hot out here. Are you sure there's ice caves out here?"

"Yeah," Eduardo said. "I've seen them. And the temperature in
them never gets above 31 degrees. Hard to believe, isn't it? Ice caves
in the Valley of the Fires." He handed Bronwynn his water bottle.

Bronwynn chugged down several swallows and handed the bottle back to him. "I don't think I like desert camping. Everything either bites or stabs you. My socks are full of cactus spines. And the landscape looks like Mars or something. Look at my boots. The rocks have cut them up so bad I'll have to walk back barefoot."

Eduardo looked down at his own boots. They were gouged and cut from their walk as if a madman with a razor had slashed out at his feet. "Yeah, it's a rough hike, but seeing this cave will be worth the scratches and blistered skin. Think about it. How many people have ever seen an ice cave in the middle of a desert? And I'll get some great photos and a good magazine article out of it."

"What will we get?" Bronwynn asked.

"An unforgettable adventure and my gratitude for your company," Charles said.

"The trip's already unforgettable," Bronwynn said. "I'll never come to the desert again."

They passed through a thicket of scrub juniper and cactus skeletons and came upon a *jacal*. An old woman, her skin wizened and blackened from the sun, sat in the shade of the brush hut picking at her tangled gray hair with bony hands.

Charles waved. "Hello. We're students from the University of Texas in Austin. Do you mind if we talk to you?" The old woman stared at them but said nothing. Charles glanced at the others. "What do you make of this, Eduardo?"

"*Bruja*," he said. "She's a witch. They're the only Indians that live alone in the desert. Let's go on."

"Ah, come on," Charles said. "Let's go meet her. This might be a real photo opportunity. I'd like to meet a real witch."

"No, you wouldn't," Eduardo said.

"Maybe she's got something cool to drink," Charles said.

"That's real funny, Charles. There's hardly any water out here. That's why we're toting two gallons of water each for a two-day hike. I wouldn't eat or drink anything she offered anyway."

"Why not?" Charles said.

"Witches poison people if you've got something they want."

"What would we have that she'd want? It's hard for me to understand how you can spend all your money getting a journalism degree, yet still be eaten up with Indian superstition."

"Shut the hell up, Charles. Alright, we'll go up to her and you take your picture, but we can't stay long if we want to reach the cave before dark."

Eduardo walked up to the woman. He bowed his head slightly and greeted her in Navajo.

She shook her head. "*Soy Apache. Sientate,*" she said.

"What did she say?" Bronwynn asked.

"She's Apache," Eduardo said. "But I think she knows enough Spanish to talk to us. She said we could sit down."

They pulled off their packs, sat down in the shade near the woman, and gulped down some water from their bottles. Charles took his camera from his pack and pointed it at the woman.

The woman straightened herself and smiled, revealing a few jagged and yellow teeth. After Charles took the picture, she slumped back against the hut wall. "*Donde van?*" the woman said. She held out a rusty tin cup that Eduardo filled with water from his bottle.

"To the ice caves," Eduardo said. The woman shook her head, so he repeated himself in Spanish. "*A las cavernas del hielo.*"

The old woman nodded. "*Frio, muy frio. Lago de invierno. Lago de muertos.*"

The woman held out a basket filled with fruit-like pods. "*Quiere las tunas?*"

Charles picked out one. "*Gracias,*" he said. "Looks like prickly pear apples."

"You idiot," Eduardo whispered. "It may or may not be prickly pear. A witch can poison or drug you."

Charles took a bite. "It tastes like prickly pear. Don't be so paranoid." Charles reached into his pack and pulled out a Granola bar and handed it to the woman.

She unwrapped the bar, threw the paper to the ground, and stuffed the bar into her mouth. After wiping her mouth with her arm, she pointed to Bronwynn's ponytail. "*Damelo,*" she said. "*Damelo.*" She reached over and fingered the elastic band holding back Bronwynn's hair.

"She wants you to give her the band," Eduardo said.

Bronwynn smiled, slipped off the band and handed it to the woman, then reached into the pocket of her hiking shorts and for another band to use on her own hair. The woman grinned and pulled back the tangled mass on her head and slipped on the band. "*¿Está bien?*" she said, turning her head from side to side.

"*Está bien,*" Eduardo said. "Okay, Charles, you've met your witch. We better hit the trail." He stood up.

The woman held up a small serpent shaped stick, pointed it at a javelina skull hanging on her hut, then pointed in the direction they were going. "*No va allá,*" she said. "*Chinde, mal, mal.*"

"She says we shouldn't go to the cave," Eduardo said. "Says something about the *chinde* being there."

"*Sí, sí, chinde, chinde,*" the woman said. She raised her hands like they were claws and growled.

"What are *chinde*?" Bronwynn asked.

"Ghosts," Eduardo said. "The earth-surface dead. I'm not sure what the Apache think, but Navajos believe that when someone dies, the evil part of their spirit often returns to torment travelers and settle grudges with people they knew."

"Do you believe that crap, Eduardo?" Charles said.

"I'm half Navajo, so I guess I half believe it. Grandmother said the *chinde* killed Grandfather. One night they chased their flock of churro sheep into the desert and attacked and mutilated several of them. Grandfather went out to herd the flock back, and a *chinde* jumped out and clawed him. Gave him the ghost sickness."

"Oh, that's great, Charles, " Bronwynn said. "You've brought us to a haunted desert. What happened to your grandfather when he got this ghost sickness?"

"First, he got really sick. The family knew he was dying, so they carried him out of the hogan and laid him under his favorite shade tree. Two nights later he died. Then we brought him here to the desert and buried him near the ice cave we're going to."

"They let him die outside alone?" Bronwynn said.

"What else could they do?" Eduardo said. "He had the ghost sickness. If he had died inside, she would have had to burn the hogan to keep the evil spirit from coming back."

"But to die alone!" Bronwynn said.

"We all die alone, Bronwynn," Eduardo said. "Every culture has its demons. Navajos have the *chinde*. I guess if one demon doesn't get you, another one will."

"*Sí, sí, chinde, chinde*," the old woman said. "*Ustedes van a jornado de muertos.*"

"What did she say, Eduardo?" Bronwynn said.

"She said we're going to a dying place."

\*\*\*

AFTER they passed the next cairn, they came upon a string of *kipukas*. Past volcanic activity had chemically altered the large sandstone islands' color so that they had yellow and pink surfaces, and in other spots the sandstone had metamorphosed into giant blocks of quarts. Beyond, black volcanic rock and obsidian covered the ground. Many of the stones were green-streaked with a patina of red and purple, and the colors danced like flames in the sunlight.

They crossed a barbed wire fence, with a NO TRESPASSING sign wired to one of the old mesquite posts. "We're trespassing," Bronwynn said as they slipped through the wire.

"What the owners don't know won't hurt them," Charles said. "Besides, the NPA has prohibited access to all known ice caves, and won't even reveal their locations. It's actually good this cave's on private property. The government might not even know it exists."

When Charles heard a snort and a sharp barking sound, he looked to his left and saw several javelinas bedded down in the shade of some junipers. He stomped his foot and the pigs jumped, crashed into the brush, and vanished.

Bronwynn jumped forward and grabbed Charles' arm. "What was that?" she said.

"Javelina," Eduardo said. "They're all over this part of the country. Watch out for them. They'll tear your ass up with those long teeth."

"They didn't seem dangerous to me," Charles said. "I thought I scared them off rather easily."

"This time," Eduardo said.

Bronwynn pointed to a deer carcass under one of the junipers. "Yuk!" she said. "They were eating something dead."

"They'll eat anything," Eduardo said. "Live or dead."

At sundown, they came to a rise of ground with a tumbled mass of boulders and volcanic rock, and Eduardo set down his pack. "Okay, we're here. The cave's right up there in those rocks, by the two biggest boulders."

A thick black stream swirled from the rocks and then separated into specks that vanished into the sky.

"Look at all those birds," Bronwynn said.

"Those are bats," Eduardo said. "They live in the caves."

" Charles, you didn't say anything about bats being in this cave," Bronwynn said.

"Don't worry, they don't bite. I just hope we don't have to wade through a lot of guano. Let's go take a look at the cave," Charles said.

"Wait till tomorrow," Eduardo said. "The ground's rough and it would be easy to break a leg in the dark. There's a bunch of lava tubes up there and since I haven't been here in a long time, I'll need daylight to find the right hole to crawl into."

After a supper of crackers and sardines, Charles pulled a bottle from his pack. "Hey, I brought some mescal," Charles said. "Let's celebrate reaching the cave. You want some, Eduardo?"

"Sure. But I can't believe you'd bring that rot-gut stuff when you could have bought some perfectly good whiskey."

"Just felt mescal would fit the setting." Charles poured some into each of their cups. "Here try a sip, Bronwynn."

Bronwynn took a small swig and shuddered and handed the cup back to him. "God, it tastes like kerosene. How can you drink that?"

As darkness fell, stars blanketed the sky and the moon rose. Charles lit a lantern, and they listened to the wind as it wound its way through the brush and rock formations.

"Listen," Bronwynn said. "Sometimes the wind sounds like someone's laughing or talking. It's weird."

"Desert's a strange place. Maybe it's the *chinde*," Eduardo says. He stood, stretched his arms, and smiled. "Maybe they don't like us camping out here." He held out his cup to Charles. "How about another shot of that mescal?"

Bronwynn stood up. "Be back in a minute. I need to change out of this stinky shirt." She pulled a tee shirt out of her pack and walked to the edge of the lantern's light. She turned her back to them and peeled off the shirt. Her naked white skin glowed in the light of the lantern and the moon.

Eduardo sat down next to Charles and stared at Bronwynn. "That some woman you got there, Charles. Some woman."

"Yeah, she is." Charles quickly downed his cup of mescal and poured another.

"Not too bashful, is she?"

"Shut up, Eduardo."

When Bronwynn returned, Eduardo stood up. "I'll be back in a minute." He grinned and walked out into the brush.

"You son of a bitch," Charles said under his breath.

"Why'd you say that?" Bronwynn said. "Where's Eduardo going?"

"Who knows. Well, I'm done in. Let's get some sleep."

When Charles stood up, he staggered and nearly fell. "Whew! That mescal's pretty stout." After he recovered his balance, he and Bronwynn spread out their sleeping bags on a bare slab of sandstone. They took off their boots and lay down. Charles could feel the hardness and coarseness of the stone against his back even while he felt the softness of Bronwynn's arms around him. Some coyotes howled neared them. Charles sat up and saw two coyotes sitting on their haunches on the large boulders Eduardo said marked the entrance to the cave. Charles lay down again and when he closed his eyes, he felt like he was tumbling, and when he opened them, the stars spun wildly. "God, I hope I don't get sick," he whispered to Bronwynn. "I think this stuff is fermenting in my stomach."

"You'll be alright," Bronwynn said. "Just don't drink anymore. You always try to do too much of everything. Just quit talking and go to sleep."

\*\*\*

EDUARDO poured himself another full cup of the mescal. He drained it, then turned off the lantern and lay down on his own sleeping bag. As he began to drift into sleep, he heard a snort and felt hot breath on his face. He jerked up and saw a javelina by his bedroll. Its eyes glowed red in the moonlight and the coarse hair on its back bristled. The javelina snorted again and its nostrils flared as it popped its long front teeth. Eduardo kicked out at the javelina, grabbed a rock and hurled it. The rock struck the pig on its thick collar and ricocheted to the ground.

"Shoo, you sorry excuse for a pig. Git out of here!" Eduardo shouted.

The pig turned and ran into the brush a few feet, then stopped and turned around again.

When Eduardo jumped up and ran at the pig, it disappeared into the brush. Eduardo picked up two more rocks and followed. He threw the rocks hard at a dark spot of ground where he thought the pig might be. He heard movement, and strained his eyes to find the shape of the javelina in the shadows. Instead he saw a human shape rise and walk toward him.

"Who's there? Bruja, is it you? Even a kook like you should know better than to come into a camp at night!"

The shape stepped back into the shadows.

"Why don't you show yourself?" he shouted.

Bronwynn shook Charles.

"What is it, Bronwynn?"

"Listen. What's wrong with Eduardo?"

Charles sat up and willed his mescal-beaten eyes to focus on Eduardo who was standing and shouting at the darkness.

"God he must be really drunk," Bronwynn said. "Listen to him. Who's he talking to? Maybe the desert really does make people crazy."

"He's probably just had too much mescal. Hey! Eduardo, you okay?"

Eduardo wobbled on his feet and pointed at the desert. "A javelina came into camp and after I ran him out, I saw someone in the brush. I can't find my flashlight or I'd go out and kick their ass."

"You're drunk, Eduardo, and you're seeing things," Charles said. "No one's out here."

Eduardo sat down on his sleeping bag, still looking out into the dark. "I tell you someone's outside our camp. I can hear him moving in the brush now. Right behind me. Put your light on them."

Charles stood, turned on his flashlight, and scanned the ground behind Eduardo. The beam caught several pairs of red eyes close to the ground. "It's feral pigs, Eduardo. That's all it was."

Eduardo picked up another rock and threw it. The herd of javelinas squealed and snorted and ran wildly away from the camp. Charles followed them with the beam of the MAG-LITE. The herd stopped for a moment as another one joined them and then they vanished into the desert night.

*** 

Charles woke in the gray twilight of dawn, shook out his boots to make sure they contained no scorpions or snakes, and made coffee. Eduardo lay sprawled on the bare ground, the empty bottle of mescal in his hand. Charles sipped his coffee and watched the sun rise, and when the soft reds of the dawn sky disappeared into an explosion of light, he woke Bronwynn and Eduardo.

"Up and at'em, campers. Let's get on to this cave." He took each a cup of coffee.

Eduardo sat up. "I don't know if I can get up."

"Maybe it's true what they say about Indians and firewater."

"Screw you, Charles. Got any aspirin?"

They ate a breakfast of oatmeal and orange drink and enjoyed the cool of the desert morning. Then Eduardo led them to a pair of basalt boulders near the mouth of the cave.

Charles glanced at the towering rock surface and smiled. "Look, petroglyphs." Carefully etched onto the smooth surface of the stones were geometric symbols, a seven-foot horned rattlesnake, a javelina, and several masked people. "You didn't tell me about this, Eduardo."

"I'd forgotten about them."

"How could you forget something like this?" Charles said.

Bronwynn put her finger on one of the human figures and snickered. "Look, he's anatomically correct. So what tribe of Indians lived out here?"

"The Jornodo Morgollón," Charles said. "Most of them were eaten by the volcano that made this valley and the ice caves. I don't know if they were the ones that made these though."

"What does Jornodo Morgollón mean?" Bronwynn asked.

"The stupid ones," Eduardo said. "No one in their right mind would live out here. My father and grandfather came to the ice cave once or twice a year. I always hated it when they brought me with them. But they said there was big medicine here and that I needed to make peace with the desert."

Charles smiled. "Did you?"

"No."

Charles laughed and after he finished taking pictures of the petroglyphs, Eduardo pointed to a small hole in the ground near the boulders.

"There's your ice cave entrance," Eduardo said.

"That little hole is a cave?" Bronwynn said.

"It's a lava tube, and it's deep. It gets a little wider once you're inside."

"How far down is the ice?" Bronwynn said.

"Seems like we crawled an hour or so before we reached the ice."

"Let's go in," Charles said. "I want to be first." Charles stuck his head inside, turned on his mag light and peered down the shaft. After he put on his leather gloves, he slid down the lava vent feet first. He felt the jagged and rough surface of the lava against his legs. A few yards down the tube widened. "So far, so good," Charles said. "The slant is not too bad. You two might as well come on. Be careful. The rocks are sharp."

Eduardo and Bronwynn joined him, and they crept slowly down the lava tube. The cramped size of the tunnel slowed down their progress. As they went deeper, the temperature gradually decreased, and in spite of the exertion of moving, Charles felt chilled. The cave widened into a large room and there they found the ice. A thick layer covered the walls, floor, and ceiling of the cave. Charles had heard that the ice in some caves was up to twenty feet thick. The ice had a blue-green tint and the color reminded Charles of the color of the ocean. "Look at how blue the ice is, Bronwynn, blue as your eyes, bluer than the sky."

"I thought it would look more like Carlsbad Caverns and have ice cycles," Bronwynn said. "I'm cold now. How long do we have to stay in this icebox?"

"You two can go back to the camp if you want, but I've got a lot of work to do here. This is fantastic," Charles said. "Do you know how old this ice is?" He pulled his camera, tape measure, and note pad out of his daypack.

"I'm ready to go too," Eduardo said.

"So go. I'll be up later."

"Better hurry, it will be dark soon," Eduardo said.

\*\*\*

EDUARDO woke with a start. He heard something moving through the brush. He stood and swept the camp with his flashlight. Bronwynn was asleep on her sleeping bag, but there was no sign of Charles. He scanned the ground around the camp and the beam of light caught three pairs of red eyes glowing close to the ground. "Shoo!" he hissed. The eyes vanished. He turned around and saw an old man standing near him, his skin black in the moonlight, his clothes ragged and soiled.

"The others said you would come back here."

Eduardo recognized the voice.

"Grandfather?"

"Yes." He nodded and held out his arms as if to embrace him.

Eduardo shrank back. "No, stay away!" A putrid smell of decaying flesh wafted his way. The old man's eyes were malignant spots with a red glow, like the eyes of people in a night-flash photograph.

"You must come with us, Eduardo. Do not fear me. Am I not your grandfather?" He laughed, and then slapped Eduardo.

Eduardo felt long nails dig into his face. He shouted for Charles and Bronwynn then turned and ran into the brush, blindly trying to make his way through the thorny scrub. Cactus and rocks slashed at his bare feet, and he felt them wet and warm with his blood. He saw red eyes around him, dozens of them, and suddenly something tripped him. He fell and slammed his face into the hard ground and lost consciousness.

\*\*\*

BRONWYNN woke when she heard Eduardo scream. "Eduardo!" she whispered loudly. "What's wrong?" When he didn't answer, she picked up the flashlight and moved toward the cave entrance to call for Charles, but in the dark she couldn't tell which hole in the ground belonged to the ice cave. She heard laughter and voices around her. "Who's there?" she shouted. "You better leave me alone!" More laughter. When she heard something scrambling over the rocks behind her, she ran back toward their camp. Someone jumped in front of her and threw dirt in her face. "Leave me alone," she screamed. She turned to run, but a rough hand grabbed her leg and tripped her. Suddenly she felt a dozen hands pulling at her clothes and hair and clawing her skin with sharp nails. She struggled to free herself, but the hands only gripped her more fiercely. She looked up and saw Eduardo's leering face above her, a knife in his hand. Then, all she could see was blackness.

\*\*\*

Charles finished his last roll of film, made some final notes, put a small sample of the ice into a jar, and began the long crawl back to the surface. He rolled out of the opening and walked into camp. Neither Bronwynn nor Eduardo were in their sleeping bags. "Hey," he shouted. "Eduardo! Bronwynn!" He sat down on his sleeping bag and lit the lantern, wondering where they could be. Then he heard Bronwynn's voice.

" Charles, I'm over here." Bronwynn walked into the clearing. Her shirt was shredded, and her face, legs, and arms were cut and scratched and the blood had dried in long streaks on her white skin.

"What happened to you?" he asked. "Where's Eduardo? Did he do this?"

She laughed. "Eduardo's out there, with the others. Did you have fun playing in your little cave?"

"I don't know what's happened, but you're talking crazy. We've got to get you out of here and find a doctor."

"What? No kiss?" She walked to him, kissed him, then bit his lip hard. "How's that? You always said I was a good kisser."

He pushed her back and touched his bloody lip with his fingers. "What the hell is wrong with you?" He heard laughter behind them in the brush. He whirled around and the beam of his flashlight caught the shapes of several people—Mexican vaqueros, Indians, Anglo cowboys—all with splotched and rotten skin, leering eyes, and jagged teeth, men who had traveled too far into the desert alone.

"Shit! We gotta get out of here." He grabbed Bronwynn's arm. "Where's Eduardo? We need him to find our way back!"

"He's dead, Silly."

Eduardo stepped out from the shapes and pushed Charles roughly out of the way. Bronwynn placed her arms around Eduardo and kissed him.

"MMMMM," she said. "At last, Eduardo's paying me some attention."

"What the hell do you think you're doing?" Charles shouted.

Eduardo released Bronwynn and busted Charles across the face with his fist. Charles staggered, turned, and ran back toward the cave. He heard laughter and sounds of pursuing footsteps. He plunged headfirst into the small hole, but several hands grabbed his legs and dragged him face down across the rocks back into the brush. When the hands released him, he looked up into the face of Eduardo. An old Indian man stood beside him.

" Charles, I'd like for you to meet my grandfather," Eduardo said.

"You're Eduardo's grandpa?"

The old man nodded.

"I'm not going to get out of this one, am I?" Charles said.

The old man shook his head and grinned. A white man with a scabbed and bloody face joined them. In one hand he carried four sharpened sticks, and in the other hand held Eduardo's coil of rope.

"Hell," Charles says. The white man lassoed Charles' neck and dragged him up deeper into the brush.

\*\*\*

At sundown the next day, the Apache woman stood over Charles. He had been staked out spread-eagle to the ground. Ants covered much of his body and thorns and cactus spines had been pressed deep into his white flesh. The mutilated bodies of Bronwynn and Eduardo lay on either side of him. She stripped the bodies of their clothes and emptied their backpacks on the ground and filled one of the packs with everything she wanted. She looked toward the cave and saw the two coyotes sitting on their haunches by the entrance, and the bats rising from the dark holes of the earth into the sky. The wind stirred and she heard the malignant whispers of the *chinde* and knew they were near. For protection, she fingered the amulet pouch around her neck, a pouch containing the gall bladders of a bear, coyote, and deer. Charles moaned loudly, and she heared the herd of javelinas crashing through the brush toward him. "*Sí, sí, chinde, chinde. Voy,*" she said. She rose, and dragging the heavy pack, hurried back toward her *jacal* while the javelinas fed on the three travelers.

# Green Irish Eyes

"It's a version of history you won't find in the books, Neil," Seamus said. "The arm of Sinn Fein is long and bloody. Now, Frankie there, he would know. He's from Belfast. Was a runner for the People's Army. Hey, Frankie!"

Frankie looked up from his mopping.

"When you get a minute, come here and meet my friend Neil. A good Irish boy himself, he is."

"Be right with you, Seamus." Frankie took a drag of the cigarette hanging from his mouth, pulled up the sleeve of his long-sleeve T-shirt above his elbow. A dragon was tattooed on his arm and elbow. As he lifted the cigarette to his mouth, his muscles flexed and the dragon seemed to come to life and roar and the Irish tri-color flag flapped in the dragon's mouth.

I was not surprised Seamus had a worker who had been with the IRA. Seamus' pub was an Irish fist in the face of Jackson's yuppies and bluebloods. On the wall were framed photographs of Michael Collins, Stephen Plunkett, Brendan Behan; there were posters and other ephemera—a tile from the roof of Michael Collin's house, a Sniper at Work sign taken from a C'maglen street corner, a library marker written in Gaelic.

I held out my hand when Frankie came to our table. "Seamus said you were in the IRA. What did you do?"

Frankie glanced at Seamus, and then shrugged his shoulders. "They called me a go-to guy. Sent me to make small weapons drops and messages. What's it to you?"

The bluntness of tough Irish boys always catches me by surprise, and I sat there thinking of how to answer.

"Don't get pissy, Frankie. He's as Irish as we are," Seamus said. "Neil is a songwriter with a true gift for words."

Frankie nodded. "Well, he and I will have a good talk sometime if he'll buy the drinks. Have you seen Morgan?"

"She'll be here later tonight."

"When you see her, tell her I'll be out with Tommy tonight. We're going to check out a new club in Mound."

"You want me to tell my daughter that her fiancée is going to a strip club?"

"Naw. Just tell her I'm going out. We'll talk later, Neil."

Seamus said, "Do you know my daughter, Morgan, Neil?"

I nodded.

"She's a lucky girl to meet a guy like Frankie here. How about you? Do you have a sweetheart?"

"There's a girl . . . let's just say the first time I saw her she took my breath away."

"Does she feel the same?" Seamus asked.

"I don't know for sure. I'd like to think so."

Frankie said, "I better get back to work, Seamus."

"Aye." Seamus reached out and squeezed Frankie's arms. "Would you look at those muscles, Neil. He's got the arms of an Olympic weightlifter. Best bouncer I ever had."

That's when I really squirmed.

*** 

As the weather was mild, I left the bar for a table on the covered patio. Morgan strolled into the club about eight. A natural beauty, she carried her slender frame with an air of ease and confidence. Her long red hair was pulled back under a ball cap with Gaelic lettering on it, and she wore a maroon sweatshirt and jeans. As I hoped, she sat down at my table.

"How about a beer, Neil?" she said.

"Sure." I signaled Mary, the waitress, as she bustled by our table. "We'll each have a pint and a glass."

The Conleys had launched into another song, and the singer's voice sounded very Irish, though as far as I knew, he had never been to Ireland. He pounded his bodhran with a tempo that matched my heart.

Mary returned with our drinks and we lifted our shot glasses. "To Ireland," I said. "And to a beautiful lady."

"To Ireland, and a handsome man," she replied. "And to other things."

112

We drained the shots and we sipped our beers. A little bit of froth from the stout clung to her lips, and she licked it off. It was difficult to not stare and lose myself in those green eyes.

"What are you looking at?" she asked.

"Your eyes." I quoted a few lines of a poem by Frances Collins:

> *So stir the fire and pour the wine,*
> *And let those sea-green eyes divine,*
> *Pour their love-madness into mine.*

"I like that poem. I'll take your reciting it as a compliment. Eyes are not usually what a guy notices."

"Shakespeare called eyes the windows of the heart, and others have said that beauty enters the soul through the eyes. Okay, sorry. I'm rattling. You're just so cute you make me stupid."

She laughed. "How do you like my cap?" she asked.

"I like it fine."

"What does it say? I can't read Gaelic."

"It says, *Kiss Me, I'm Irish.*"

"Okay," she said. She leaned over and kissed me. One of her girlfriends hooted. Morgan gave her the finger.

I heard Seamus call out, "Morgan!"

"Be right there," she said. "Well, I've got to help my father tonight. He's a little short on help. Thanks for the drink. I'll send Mary out with another Guinness—on me."

When Morgan left, I moved to another table so I could see inside the bar. She had slung a towel on her shoulder and stuck a bottle opener in her back jeans pocket and as the crowd was picking up, she scurried about from table to table, picking up dishes, wiping off tables, and taking orders. I joined the line at the men's room. As she walked from the bar into the kitchen, she passed me, touched my middle-aged waist with her hand and said, "Wish we could talk more, but it's really busy. I'll have to catch you later. How about tomorrow night?"

"I'll be here." I walked out to the car whispering, *Stupid . . . moron . . . what are you doing?*

The next night, I was back at my table. Seamus nodded when he saw me, but didn't stop to bullshit like he usually did. I thought he was just busy till I saw him sitting at the bar gabbing with a few of the customers at the bar. When I saw Morgan, I forgot about Seamus, about Frankie, about anything but her. She stopped at the edge of the patio entrance and smiled when she saw me. She was a striking tableau in her high heels, black pants, and a black tank-type shirt and jacket. Silver earrings dangled from her ears and her hair was pulled into a ponytail.

I waved, like a completely smitten and undone simpleton, and when she made it to my table, I stood and pulled back a chair so she could sit.

We drank more than we should have. She reached for my hand and squeezed it. I melted, and she knew it.

"Let's go for a drive," she said.

She stood and led me by the hand outside. We took my car and drove to the post office where she mailed some letters. I noticed that at least one was addressed to someone in Maze Prison in Northern Ireland. From there we went to the Wildlife Refuge and looked at the moon and shooting stars. I followed the trail of one heavenly monster as it sliced through the blackness and found myself looking into her eyes.

"We really shouldn't do this," she said.

"I know, but I don't think I can stop myself."

"I know."

We kissed, and then I said, "You know what I'd like to do? I'd like to take you to Ireland someday. I want to be away from Jackson, in a world all our own. I want to kiss you whenever I want, to walk down the street holding your hand. I want to belong to you and I want you to belong to me.

She sighed. "I'd like that too."

"I found a writer, a Madame Delphine Gay de Girardin, who said, 'A woman whom we truly love is a religion.' I think she was right. And I think you're my religion."

"Enough daydreaming and pretty words, English professor. We know what we're here for."

The next day, Morgan called me. "We've got to talk, Neil."

"Okay, I—"

"No, listen. I'm not up to you breaking my heart. I like you—a lot—but I'm not going to see you anymore if it's not going to go anywhere."

"I don't know about you, Morgan, but I'm not going anywhere. I'm sure I'm in love with you."

"You say that now, but you really don't know. Let's give each other a week's space. If I don't hear from you, then I'll know for sure. It will hurt me, and you might hurt some too, but if we handle it now, it'll be manageable. We would have real problems anyway."

"You mean with Frankie?"

"Yes, and with my father too. He wouldn't handle it well. You'd be losing a friend."

"You'd be worth any price."

"We'll see. Goodbye, Neil. One week."

I avoided Seamus and the pub all the next week. Sat around the house and drank mostly. The week finally passed, but when the deadline to call her came, I sat and looked at the phone, unplugged it, and went to bed. The next night I drank half a fifth of Bushmill's while I looked at the phone, passed out, and barely made it to the university in time to teach my 8:00 class. I felt as paralyzed as a Prufrock. The next night, I drank the other half of the Bushmills. In spite of my self-medication, I didn't sleep well that night, and in a hypnagogic state I realized that I couldn't let her go. The devil take Frankie and Seamus. If Seamus were a true friend, I figured he'd get over it and he'd help Frankie get over it too. Frankie had more important things to do than to fool with me anyway—like going to strip clubs and killing British soldiers and such.

I called Morgan every hour the next day, but there was no answer. I called the bar and asked Mary if she had seen Morgan.

"No," she said. "She and Frankie left for New Orleans. I think they're going to catch a plane to Ireland."

I opened another bottle of Bushmills, filled a glass, and sat down to think. Only two days late. I flipped through the cable stations looking for a movie to take my mind off of Morgan. It must have been Irish Day or something. *The Devil's Own, In the Name of the Father,*

*Patriot Games, The Crying Game*—none of them suited my mood at the time.

I heard my back door open. Maybe it was the whiskey, but I said it anyway. "Morgan?"

"No, I'm not Morgan, lad," a male voice said. The accent was thick with Irish.

I started to get up from my chair, but a vice-like hand pushed me down. "Just sit right there, lad."

I looked at him. He was middle-aged, wore a stocking cap, a thick gray sweater covered by an old British field jacket, and camouflage pants. "Who are you and what are you doing in my house?"

"My name is Lorcan, a friend of the family you might say."

"You mean Seamus?"

"I do. Hell, you're brighter than they said you were. Well, Neil, you've created quite a problem, and I've been sent to fix that."

"Are you with the Ira?"

"That I am. Of course, if I told you that, I'd have to kill you."

"I don't care who you are. Get your ass out." I rose from my chair but his fist hammered my nose and knocked me back down.

"Now, don't irritate me. Look at you, a bloody mess you are." He tossed me a handkerchief. "Wipe your nose, and take yourself another drink of that good Irish whiskey."

While I chugged down the whiskey, I watched him open a jacket's bag slung over his shoulder and fish out a roll of duct tape, a pistol, and a Black and Decker drill. When I set down the bottle he tightly bound my feet and arms with the tape. "Why are you doing this?" I asked.

"You can't go around breaking a young Irish girl's heart now, can you, laddie. And you insulted your friend Seamus by sneaking around with her like you did. Did you think that Seamus wouldn't notice you were seeing his daughter? And Frankie, he's not one to piss off either."

"Well, tell Seamus I'm sorry. Just have Frankie come over and kick my ass. I'll make it up to him."

"Sorry, laddie. My orders were clear—kneecap you, both legs, then one bullet to the head." He taped my mouth shut, held up the drill, and spun the bit. "Now, what is it the doctor says? This is going to sting a little bit."

Actually, it hurt a great deal, but the pain in my heart screamed almost as loud as I did when the drill bit into my knee. I didn't even think about how bad the pain was. I had always thought my last thoughts would be significant, peaceful—that they would be emotionally charged, summing up my life, finally fitting together all the jagged pieces of the puzzle—that I would find clarity and meaning in the tragedies, the losses, the failures—even failures like this one. But my thoughts weren't about those things at all.

All I could think about was Morgan—and I relieved the dreams I had experienced since the first time I had seen her. I imagined her kiss, the softness of her hands, of walking with her in Ireland. My last conscious thought was how lost I was in those green eyes. And my conscience whispered some lines from a Longfellow poem:

> *A pretty girl, and in her tender eyes*
> *Just that soft shade of green we sometimes see*
> *In evening skies.*

# Clean Nets

Ever since Indian Territory days, my family has fished this Red River. Mama always said there ain't no call for us to be ashamed of it neither. She says the first apostles were fishermen, and that if fishermen are good enough for Jesus, then the rest of the world will just have to accept us too.

When they finished the Lake Texoma Dam in 1944, the Red River changed, and our family had to change with it. Now, most of our fishing time is spent on the lake. We also started guiding some, helping those tourists with more money than sense to catch sand bass or stripers, or get them to some ducks and geese in hunting season. They're surprised we ain't got no fish sonar or duck radar or fancy gear like that. We just know where the fish are and where the ducks like to go. Ain't really much to it if a man pays attention.

The life of a fisherman ain't as simple as it used to be. Now I gotta fool with getting all kinds of permits. My daddy fishes with us some. He still cain't read, so I have to read each year's new rules to him. The state says we gotta count and measure fish, and throw back the game fish if they get tangled up in my nets or traps or get on my trotlines. I have to throw them back even if they're gonna die. Seems like a waste of good fish. Sometimes I keep them anyway and take them over to Hendrix and give them away to the colored people there. I guess that's okay, long as I don't sell them. Sometimes I wonder what these state bureaucrats are thinking. If they'd just talk to a fisherman, they'd get lots of ideas. But I reckon they don't care for talking to someone who knows how to do something they are passing laws for. No one used to pay us fishermen much mind. Now, we get more attention than I care to have from all kinds of folks, but mostly from rabbit rangers who seem set on catching us breaking some crazy law someone thought up.

Yet, I ain't got it as bad as some. I read one story of some fellows that got put in the pen for importing half a dozen lobsters that were an inch or so too short. The paper said that government prosecutors worked on this case for six months. Seems like six months of detective work and lawyers would have cost a passel of tax dollars to prosecute this lobtsergate conspiracy. I hope they don't get so desperate to keep a job that they would pick on poor fishermen like myself.

We make most of our money off the catfish we sell, but I noticed it's getting harder to sell them. People are getting attached to that pond-raised catfish, or lately, that catfish or tapia that comes frozen all the way from China. But they don't taste the same as river fish. Anyone raised on river fish can tell you that.

But what a lot of folks don't know is that we got all kinds of good fish here, not just catfish. There's brim, largemouth bass, crappie, gar, drum, buffalo, carp, black bass, sand bass, stripers, hybrids (I reckon a hybrid happens when a sand bass gets to know a striper real well), and spoonbill catfish that we snag down by the dam when the rabbit rangers ain't around. We eat'em all too.

But even though I spend a good bit of my fishing time on Lake Texhoma, and she works me near to death, I still love that damned old Red River. She's toned down some since the dam was finished, but she's still got a mind of her own. She don't flood much no more, like she did when she devoured the town of Karma, north of Bonham where my grandma had a store. Grandma told me how she and my grandpa just watched the river warsh the whole town away. Weren't nothin' they could do bout it. And there ain't nothin' lives there now. Lady Red must not have liked that town much.

The river used to have a bunch of logjams, but they're pretty much all gone now. Daddy said that in his day the logs were so thick you could walk across the river and never get your feet wet. The river's still got quicksand, even though it ain't as bad as it was. I don't know where it went to, but only a few spots are bad to have it now. People who don't know about quicksand or can't spot it are in bad shape if they get caught in it alone. It must be horrible for someone to get drownded in mud, being sucked down to the river's bottom. I only got in quicksand once. Daddy hauled me out and told me how the last person he pulled out of quicksand was a woman, and he had to reach down and pull her out by the hair. She was real dead, he said. And then after making me take a close look at the quicksand, he whipped my little ass with a willow switch real good so I'd remember not to come near it again. I learnt right then what quicksand looked like and I ain't stepped into it since. A good thrashin' always helps the memory.

When the water's high enough, I load up the kids and their grandaddy on the johnboat or airboat, and take them downriver, explaining to them all they need to know 'bout the river nowadays. When the water's too low for a boat, I walk its banks on Sundays. Sunday is the only day I don't fish; it's the only day our family ever took off from work. I find stuff—old bottles, lots of trash that I guess came down from the dam, 'cause I sure don't see no people around to leave it there. Sometimes I think the river's got a mind of her own and just puts things where she wants when she's tired of playing with it.

Mama says the river used to be haunted. Gave people some kind of fever that made them start killing folks. Ever time some good ole boy goes on a killin' rampage, Mama says that the fever's come back to the Red River Valley. "If'n you ever see someone who don't belong down there, you be real careful," she says. "Look at their eyes. The ones with the fever got the same look as a wild dog that ain't afraid of humans no more."

"How do people get well from this fever, Mama?" I asked.

"Ain't but one cure," she said. "They got to be put down, just like they's a rabid dog."

I think that fever's been around now and then because my family's found several dead bodies on the river or in the lake through the years. Drownings mostly. Some of them could swim, but they underestimated the strength of the current and the temperamental nature of the river. Sometimes I think she just don't care for people thrashing around in her and gets riled up and pulls them down. Some of the others I just don't know how they got there cause they still got their shoes and fancy city clothes on. You can tell they didn't fall off no boat.

My house ain't far from the Carpenter's Bluff Bridge. We see folks down there in summer swimming and diving off the bridge. They go there at night too and build fires and drink and all. I couldn't sleep one night and I floated down river, sittin' in the front of the boat just sculling along, and I saw a bunch of folks underneath the bridge. They was sitting in the light of a campfire and I heard them carrying on.

Sounded like they were having a big time. When she's a mind to, the river knows how to make folks real happy and feel like they belong there. Only difference between these visiting folks and me is that I belong on the river all the time.

My wife Sophie and I had us a bunch of kids, and all of them know how to fish. The littlest ones we teach to get bait. They seine crawfish out of ponds and ditches, dig worms, seine minners out of the creek and sell them so they can have some spending money. But I only got one out of the bunch that's taken to fishing enough that I know he'll be a fisherman all his life. When he ain't in school, he's with me. Elvin's a tough one—you can tell by his callused little hands. He doesn't cry when he gets wet or cold. He don't mind getting his face blistered by the wind or sun. He works right beside me until the fish are all cleaned and we get everything ready for the next day.

One day we was warshin' and mending our nets and he says, "You must have the cleanest nets in the river, Daddy. Why you warsh them so much?"

"Dirty nets don't catch no fish, boy." Then I tell him what my daddy always told me. "When Jesus called them first apostles, they was warshing nets when he found them. So right away he called them to follow him, 'cause he knew they were good fishermen. They kept fishing too, only from then on they fished for men. A man's got to keep his nets clean in life, boy, if'n he wants anything in them but trash."

We was on the river one afternoon and my boy was walking the sandbars and stepped into some quicksand. I hauled him out of it and whipped his little butt with a willow switch, just like my daddy done me. And I explained to him how the river, she don't cotton to a man bein' careless. He's got to pay attention all the time. I told him how the river's different now, and how she'll be different when he's growed up too. Maybe then she won't have no quicksand at all, but she does now, and he cain't go messin' around in it.

I don't know why my family likes fishing so. I guess we were just meant to do it. But I know when I feel that tug on my line, and I feel that life there, it feels real good. And when I can sell a pickup load of iced-down catfish to the grocers, and go back home with money, it makes me feel good to buy my family things they need. Good fishing goes in spells, so I don't always catch as much as I want. Sometimes the river pushes the fish away from us just to see if we love her enough to stick with her. She ain't run us off yet. Hell, we ain't goin' nowhere.

# RICKEY E. PITTMAN
# THE BARD OF THE SOUTH

## Author, Storyteller, Songwriter, & Folksinger

Rickey E. Pittman, the Bard of the South, is a storyteller, author, and folksinger, was the Grand Prize Winner of the 1998 Ernest Hemingway Short Story Competition, and is originally from Dallas, Texas. Pittman presents his stories, music and programs at schools, libraries, organizations, museums, Civil War Reenactments, restaurants, banquets, and Celtic festivals throughout the South.

## Books by the Bard of the South
### Available at  http://www.bardofthesouth.com/books/

*Red River Fever*
*Under the Witch's Mark*
*Jim Limber Davis: A Black Orphan in the Confederate White House*
*Stonewall Jackson's Black Sunday School*
*The Scottish Alphabet*
*The Irish Alphabet*
*The Confederate Alphabet*
*Ariel: Therapy Dog of the Rio Grande Valley*
*The ABC Book of the Rio Grande Valley*

### *Music CDs*

*The Bard of the South*
*The Minstrel Boy by the Bard of the South*
*A Lover's Ghost*
*Osceola and Foster*

Music is available on iTunes and other online sites. To hear samples, visit: http://www.bardofthesouth.com/music